Anonymous

In Memory of the Life and Ministry of the Rev. William Pratt Breed, D.D.

Late Pastor of the West Spruce Street Presbyterian Church, Philadelphia

Anonymous

In Memory of the Life and Ministry of the Rev. William Pratt Breed, D.D.
Late Pastor of the West Spruce Street Presbyterian Church, Philadelphia

ISBN/EAN: 9783337144944

Printed in Europe, USA, Canada, Australia, Japan

Cover: Foto ©Andreas Hilbeck / pixelio.de

More available books at **www.hansebooks.com**

IN MEMORY

OF THE

LIFE AND MINISTRY

OF

THE REV. WILLIAM PRATT BREED, D.D.,

LATE PASTOR OF THE WEST SPRUCE STREET PRESBYTERIAN
CHURCH, PHILADELPHIA.

One cannot catch the outline of a hill while standing close to its foot, neither can he form a critical estimate of a human life while that life is yet in living, palpitating contact with his own.

The reader of the following papers, therefore, will not expect to find within them a cool, calm, critique of my father's life and work. This they do not profess to give. A Husband, a Father, a Brother, a Pastor, a Friend, has been taken. This little book gives voice to the sorrow and love of those who have been left. Its pages form the surface upon which scalding tears have fallen and have burned an imprint. Its words are the throbbings—the quick, hot throbbings of distressed hearts. Its lines give the articulate utterance in which the grief, hitherto inarticulate, of a family, a church, a community, struggle for expression.

Let one who was unacquainted with him of whom these papers have been written, lay them aside unread. Such a one lacks the key by which to interpret them. Let those who knew and loved my father read, and receive that ineffable comfort which flows from the utterance, by sympathetic lips, of the common sorrow of many hearts.

Milton, Penn'a, April 8th, 1890.   W. P. BREED.

SERVICES AT THE OBSEQUIES OF

REV. WILLIAM PRATT BREED, D. D.,

AT THE

WEST SPRUCE STREET PRESBYTERIAN CHURCH,

S. W. CORNER OF SPRUCE AND SEVENTEENTH STREETS,
PHILADELPHIA.

ON MONDAY, FEBRUARY 18th, 1889.

ORDER OF SERVICE.

1. ANTHEM, "I Heard a Voice," . . . . *Choir.*

2. INVOCATION, ... *Rev. Henry C. McCook, D. D.,*
Pastor of Tabernacle Presbyterian Church.

3. HYMN, No. 898, "Sun of my Soul," . . . . . . *Rev. Francis J. Collier, D. D.*

4. READING OF HOLY SCRIPTURES, ... *Rev. J. R. Miller, D. D.,.*
Editorial Superintendent, Presbyterian Board of Publication.

5. ADDRESS, ... *Rev. A. S. Freeman, D. D.,*
Of Haverstraw, N. Y.

6. ADDRESS, ... *Rev. Robert M. Patterson, D. D., LL. D.*

7. CHANT, "Beyond the Smiling and the Weeping," . . . . *Choir.*

8. PRAYER, ... *Rev. Stephen W. Dana, D. D.,*
Pastor of Walnut Street Presbyterian Church.

9. ADDRESS, ... *Rev. J. Addison Henry, D. D.,*
Pastor of Princeton Presbyterian Church.

10. ADDRESS, ... *Rev. Charles A. Dickey, D. D.,*
Pastor of Calvary Presbyterian Church.

11. HYMN, "Asleep in Jesus," . . . . *Choir.*

12. ADDRESS, ... *Rev. Henry C. McCook, D. D.,*
Pastor of Tabernacle Presbyterian Church.

13. HYMN, No. 932, "Abide with Me," . . . . *Rev. Louis F. Benson,*
Pastor of Church of Redeemer, Germantown, Pa.

14. BENEDICTION, ... *Rev. W. Brenton Greene, D. D.,*
Pastor of Tenth Presbyterian Church.

ADDRESS BY REV. A. S. FREEMAN, D.D.

Dear friends, what reminiscences crowd upon my memory as I stand here to-day; but my words are only preliminary and shall be brief. Ecclesiastically, there are present to-day those who have been more closely associated with Dr. Breed in Presbytery, in Synod, in connection with the Boards of our church, in ministerial relations with the Presbytery and with brethren of other churches in Philadelphia; but there are few among the living who have known him so long and so intimately as myself.

In the year 1837 we sat together at the same table in the school of Dr. John J. Owen, of New York, fitting for college. In the year 1839, with others of my classmates whom I see here this morning, we entered the New York University. We graduated together in 1843. We entered the ministry together, and though our paths diverged, for more than forty years we have kept up an intimate, and I may say a very familiar, correspondence. We have met as classmates for more than forty years, though not every year, at the reunion of our college class. More than two years ago, the fortieth anniversary of my own pastorate, he came to be with me, and we spent a happy Sabbath, and he remained over Monday evening and attended the social reunion of the congregation; and how he entered into all with that cheerful, pleasant humor that characterized him. Less than three weeks ago at the Alumni Dinner of the University we sat, four of us, of the Class of '43, side by side, and the President of that class sat near us. How cheerful, how bright, how humorous were his remarks on that occasion! No matter how many years have passed, when college graduates meet they are boys again together.

I have thought, dear friends, of the contrast between the occasion that

9

brings us together, and *his* presence with Christ in Heaven. Here we mourn. This family mourn. These brethren in the ministry mourn. This church is a circle of bereaved mourners. Here we weep as we look upon the face of the departed and beloved. But *there*, he who trod for so many years these streets, his erect form so familiar as he went from house to house on errands of mercy, and sympathy, and love, and cheerfulness, walks to-day the golden streets of the New Jerusalem.

We may think, as we see him in his casket, that the crown has fallen from his head, but, dear friends, the Hand that was pierced has placed the crown upon his brow. When we heard that he had departed, *we* said, " It is the day of his death," but Angels say, " It is the day of his coronation." " In my Father's house are many mansions. If it were not so, I would have told you. I go to prepare a place for you, and if I go and prepare a place "—Ah, dear friends, what does he say ? Not, " I will send an Angel or an Archangel to escort you home," but, " I will come again and receive you unto myself, that where I am there ye may be also." This Divine escort has taken home to himself the friend we loved.

I will but repeat words already read. " I would not have you to be ignorant, brethren, concerning them which are asleep "—Oh, no, the Apostle did not say " dead "—" concerning them which are asleep that ye sorrow not, even as others which have no hope. For if we believe that Jesus died and rose again, even so them also which sleep in Jesus will God bring with him."

To this family, to my brethren, to this church, to all who mourn to-day, I add only these words of the Apostle : " Wherefore comfort one another with these words."

ADDRESS BY REV. R. M. PATTERSON, D.D., LL.D.

The first passage of Scripture that flashed into my mind on hearing of the death of Dr. Breed was: "He was a good man and full of the Holy Ghost and of faith."

The words may be as unqualifiedly and as unreservedly applied to him as the inspired pen applied them at first to Barnabas.

1. Dr. Breed was a *good man* in every sense that has been put upon the word in that inspired application.

Measure his life by the moral code of the Bible, which also men of the world accept as the perfect standard; judge his words and his deeds by its rules of purity, veracity, honesty, justice; and the most unprincipled skeptics can detect in him none of those flaws which they love to find in Christians. Leave his personal immortality out of the question, consider only the unblemished reputation he has left as an influence on others, and the most irreligious of the scientific positivists would not hesitate to say: "Let me live the life and die the death of such a righteous man; and let my last end be like his."

At the end of his long life and ministry he could, in this pulpit and by the press as widely as he was known, have said without the risk of a challenge: "Finally, brethren, whatsoever things are true, whatsoever things are honorable, whatsoever things are just, whatsoever things are pure, whatsoever things are lovely, whatsoever things are of good report; if there be any virtue, and if there be any praise, think on these things. The things which ye both learned and received, and heard and saw in me, these things. do: and the God of peace shall be with you."

He was a good, *i.e.*, a large-hearted, a benevolent and gentle dispositioned man: free from envy, jealousy, malignity, censorious asperity; a genial, generous, candid man; looking for the good rather than the bad in others; condemning, but condemning tenderly, the bad where it existed; and rejoicing in all true work for his Divine Master, by whomsoever done. It was the good Barnabas who trusted the young convert Paul, and vouched for him when the Apostles were suspicious, and then worked with him, though overshadowed by him, unselfishly glad at what he and others accomplished. It was Dr. Breed's delight to encourage young men, to help them to the Lord's work, to rejoice in their success in it. The Gospel work at Antioch, imperfect though it may have been, made Barnabas glad, because he was a good man; so was Dr. Breed glad, as he learned of any and every work for the Master, whether done by him or his church, or by others and other churches.

This goodness of disposition marked all his intercourse with his brethren; not only lighting up his social conversation with a perpetual pleasantry, but toning his more formal discussions with them.

We have seen him in our deliberative bodies in seasons of high excitement, amid earnest, tempestuous debate, himself earnest; but never was he known to forget himself or heard to utter a harsh word concerning an opponent.

2. *He was full of the Holy Ghost.* The believer is a temple of the Holy Spirit. The fruits of the Spirit in the life of Dr. Breed—"love, joy, peace, long-suffering, kindness, goodness, faithfulness, meekness, temperance"—showed that the Divine presence in him was full and all pervading. His Christian character was rounded, not angular. His example might almost be appealed to as a proof of perfect sanctification in this life. He would not himself have claimed it, for those who while on earth are nearest heaven in spirit are the more humbled thereby; but we who knew him will say, that as he passed from earth to the glorified presence of his Lord, he did not need much of a transformation to prevent the dread experience of Isaiah, who, when he saw the Lord of Hosts in His glory, was compelled to cry out, "Woe is me, for I am undone, because I am a man of unclean lips, for mine eyes have seen the King, the Lord of Hosts;" or that of John, who, when he saw the same glorious One, fell at His feet as dead. The live coal had touched

Dr. Breed's lips, and his iniquity was taken away, and his sin purged. He was ready to look directly into the brightly shining face and to see with unblanched eye Him in whom he had so long and fully believed.

3. He was *full of faith*. His personal faith in Jesus for his own salvation was an assurance. Hence the perennial joyfulness and the wonderful fruitfulness of his life. And that faith was not only a saving one in his Redeemer, but an unquestioning one in the Word of God. He was a thoroughgoing believer in the revealed and inspired Bible. He could not tolerate any of the wild scholarly speculations which undermine its plenary authority. A special student of the Reformation times, too, he was devoted to the Reformed Confessions, especially the Westminster. His Calvinism and his Presbyterianism were high, extreme, overmastering. He believed in them both with all his heart. In his view they were God-revealed. He held them with singular tenacity; while his large heart embraced, in the communion of the saints, and in active work, all who loved the Lord Jesus Christ in sincerity, though they could not see eye to eye with him on all doctrinal and governmental points.

He was the John of our company; not the effeminately affectionate John of the common judgment, but the real John of Scripture, who, while loving intensely and seeking tender love, was as intensely devoted to revealed truth, and was stern in his opposition to error.

Another of our ministers who died since this year opened, on the eve of his death is reported to have clipped from a paper and read with much tenderness these verses :—

> If I should die to-night,
> My friends would look upon my quiet face
> Before they laid it in its resting place,
> And deem that death has left it almost fair ;
> And laying snow-white flowers against my hair,
> Would smooth it down with cheerful tenderness,
> And fold my hands with lingering caress—
>   Poor hands, so empty and so cold to-night !

If I should die to-night,
My friends would call to mind with loving thought
Some kindly deeds the icy hands had wrought,
Some gentle word the frozen lips had said,
Errands on which the willing feet had sped;
The memory of my selfishness and pride,
My hasty words, would all be put aside,
    And so I should be loved and mourned to-night!

    If I should die to-night,
E'en hearts estranged would turn once more to me,
Recalling other days remorsefully;
The eyes that chill me with averted glance
Would look upon me as of yore, perchance,
And soften in the old familiar way,
(For who could war with dumb, unconscious clay?)
    So I might rest forgiven of all to-night!

    O friends, I pray to-night
Keep not your kisses for my dead cold brow;
The way is lonely, let me feel them now.
Think gently of me; I am travel worn;
My faltering feet are pierced with many a thorn;
Forgive, O hearts estranged, forgive, I plead!
When dreamless rest is mine, I shall not need
    The tenderness for which I long to-night!

That was an experience which Dr. Breed had not. The cases are rare, indeed, in which a man can be positive in his opinions and honest in their expression, without suffering alienations of friends and incurring the enmity of opponents. Dr. Breed *was* one of the rare cases. His convictions were strong. He expressed them strongly. He did not avoid controversy when truth required it. But there was something in him and about him which not only bound old friends to him as with bands of steel, but held the respect and good will of those from whom he differed. I cannot imagine that any recollection of alienations or wistful thought of needed reconciliation saddened his last moments.

And I do not suppose the man lives who has the pang that would now flow from the recollection of ever having spoken a harsh word about him or done an unkind deed to him.

Many a circle has been broken by this departure—nay, not broken—enlarged; for "in that kingdom where there will be neither marrying nor giving in marriage, I think there will be wedded affection, for though the nature be glorified, yet it is human nature still."

Farewell, then, brother beloved; tried and trusty friend; wise and safe counsellor; enthusiastic Presbyterian Churchman; earnest and evangelical preacher; tender and sympathetic pastor; devoted husband; exemplary parent; loyal servant of Jesus Christ. It is well with thee. Thou hast fought a good fight. Thou hast finished thy course. Thou hast kept the faith. Thou art crowned. Thy sleeping body is here, waiting to be hidden away from human eyes, until the Resurrection morn, in the bed that was sanctified by the resting therein of the body of thy crucified and risen Redeemer. It quietly and happily slept itself away after a beautiful old age. But thou, spirit-born, believing, good soul, made perfectly holy, hast entered into the joy of thy Lord. Thou hast already met many whom thou didst in this church, in Steubenville, and elsewhere, bring to Jesus, and whom, by thy preaching and pastoral work and thy writings, thou didst comfort and build up in the faith; and brethren in the ministry with whom thou didst hold sweet converse and pray and labor, and who had gone before. We hope to follow and meet thee again. Farewell for a little while—*a little while.*

ADDRESS BY REV. J. ADDISON HENRY, D.D.

Dear friends, what a different scene this is from that which many of us witnessed here some seven or eight years ago, at the time of Dr. Breed's twenty-fifth anniversary as the pastor of this church. That was a scene of joy and gladness. This house was then filled to the overflowing with those who had come to offer their congratulations, and to speak words of kindness to this dear pastor. He was surrounded by the ministry, he was also surrounded by his elders; an eldership which any minister in this city, or anywhere, might be proud to have around him. He was here, also, taken by the hand by his congregation, and by a great many friends who belonged to other churches. But this is an hour of quietness, of silence; it is an occasion of great solemnity and even of sadness, and yet it is the hour of our triumph, because another of the brethren has "overcome" through Jesus Christ our Lord. He has "fought the good fight, he has finished his course, he has kept the faith, and henceforth there is laid up for him a crown of righteousness which the Lord, the righteous Judge, shall give him at that day."

But why should I be called upon to say anything here, or why should any of these brethren be called upon to say anything that would tend to add to the estimation in which the beloved character that has passed from us is already held in your minds and hearts. I am certain we can say nothing that will add to the admiration which you already have for this noble man, and I do not know why we should say anything, other than it is well for us to speak of the virtues and of the piety of the ministers of Christ and the servants of the Cross, when they pass away from our sight forever.

I was last Saturday afternoon in the study of my dear friend, the Rev. Dr. Sands, the pastor of the Arch Street Church, and he had upon the mantel-piece of his study a picture of Dr. Breed, and under this

photograph he had written a verse from some favorite poem. I admired
the selection very much, and I have it here in my hand, for my brother
said to me " Henry, you can take it with you; " but I had no idea at
that time of using it upon this occasion—for I had not then been asked
to make this address ; but I will read these lines which Dr. Sands had
placed under the picture of our mutual friend—

> " They never quite leave us, our friends who have passed
>   Through the shadows of death to the sunlight above ;
> A thousand sweet memories are holding them fast
>   To the places they blessed with their presence and love."

Ah, friends, I am quite sure that Dr. Breed's name will be a household word in every family in this congregation, and also in every Presbyterian Church, at least in this city; and in many of the families of
those belonging to sister denominations.

I first saw Dr. Breed a good while ago. If you will forgive a
personal allusion, I will say when I was in the first year of my Theological Seminary course in Princeton, it may have been in the last year
of my college course, it was, however, just after this congregation had
entered this beautiful house of worship, and soon after they had called
Dr. Breed to be their pastor, that I happened to be one Sabbath day in
Philadelphia ; I was told, by a venerable elder, at whose house I was
staying, " You must go, my young friend, and hear Dr. Breed preach
this afternoon," and so I came to this church and sat somewhere near
where that third column is yonder upon my left, and I heard Dr. Breed
preach. He was then in his full vigor, and he delivered a most impressive sermon from the text, " The harvest is passed, the summer is ended,
and I am not saved." Those of you who have listened to the voice of
Dr. Breed again and again, will know how he dwelt on those last
words; " I am not saved." They are ringing in my ears yet. I was
so impressed by that discourse that I went to my home and made
a short synopsis of it, and in looking over my treasures a short time

2

ago, I came across that little sheet on which I had written the synopsis of that sermon. All this must have been about thirty-two years ago.

Yes, my friends, he was an impressive man; and he was a man who was complete in almost every respect. He was a remarkable man; for he was a theologian, he was a historian, I think we can honestly say he was a scientist, he was a poet, he was a humorist; and he was a faithful pastor.

Those of you who recall the little speeches that he made in the Ministerial Association will testify that what I have said is true of this beloved man. He was an excellent man, he was a good man, but he was also, as we believed in the ministry, a man of distinguished learning and acquirements.

You recollect, brethren of the ministry, that last paper which he read, just two weeks ago this very day, at No. 1334 Chestnut street, upon "Ancient Oratory," and more especially upon "Demosthenes ' *For the Crown.*'" What a paper that was! and I am sure the brethren who are before me now will say they entered into the feeling of the remark of one of the gentlemen who followed Dr. Breed when he said: "Who but our own Breed could have written such a paper as that?"

What pathos there was in every word that he spoke. There was a peculiar tenderness in his voice, and it seems to me that that tenderness grew upon certain occasions, especially during seasons of remarkable religious awakening. Did you ever hear Dr. Breed speak at a meeting where there was unmistakable evidence of the presence of the Spirit of God? If so, you were touched with the peculiar tenderness of his tones. Those of us who were members of the old Synod of Philadelphia will recollect his earnest appeals at the meetings which were held in connection with this Synod; as for instance, at Lewistown, Lewisburg, Jersey Shore, Easton, Pittston and Lock Haven. We well know how every word that that good man uttered went to the hearts of the ministry as well as to the hearts of the people.

What a sympathizing man he was! How generous, how noble in every respect; how he wanted to aid his brethren in the ministry whenever he could, not only in this city, but elsewhere. Who ever came with a strong appeal to Dr. Breed but met with a ready response? His congregation knew that very well. He opened their hearts when making an appeal, and their purses also. He would listen to the men as they came from the East and the West, from the North and from the South, and from the ends of the earth. It seemed to be impossible for Dr. William P. Breed to turn anybody away.

How many missionaries will miss this man? how they will miss the sympathy, tenderness and the gifts that have been sent from this congregation through the influence of this dear brother.

Last week I had a letter from a minister who is at present in this city. I refer to the Rev. Prof. Bertrand, of Paris, who is representing the cause of French Evangelization in this country, and he seemed to be somewhat low-spirited, because he had not been able to gain admission to many of the churches to present this worthy object, and as he had heard of the death of Dr. Breed he writes: "Dr. Breed was to help me in my confusion and my troubles." Ah! that was always true of Dr. Breed; wherever there was one in confusion or in trouble he had a friend in that man.

I could speak for hours in regard to him, but I must close these remarks. How we loved him! And must we give him up? Ah, it is too true; these elders will not have him in their meetings again. His face will not be seen in this room where the Sabbath School gathers, or in that lecture room where he met his people for the last time.

Dear Christian brethren, shall we never hear that voice in our Ministerial Association again? Must I go to my work in West Philadelphia, and to my study and prepare my sermons, and plod on in my ministerial work, and endeavor to comfort poor, sick and sorrowing humanity, and know and feel that I am never to go into that study or into the home of my dear friend and take that beloved hand into mine and look into that faithful face ? It is so ! Be still ! my soul, be still ! " Be still and know that it is God ! " " I was dumb, I opened not my mouth ; because Thou didst it."

ADDRESS OF REV. CHARLES A. DICKEY, D.D.

My dear brethren, whether we take this occasion as our opportunity for reminiscences, or whether we take it as our opportunity for presenting the character and work of Dr. Breed, it is far too short. There cannot be time enough allotted for us all to tell the stories of our friendship. There is not time to tell what we know of his fidelity. The limits of the services are properly marked, and our regard for those whose hearts are so heavily burdened, if nothing else, would deter us from much longer prolonging these services. And yet, what need is there for speech ? What is there to tell that he has not told himself? Is not his character written on our hearts ? Have we not his works and words and character and life sparkling like gems in our memories ? Has not his faithfulness recorded itself these thirty years and more in the memory of every one to whom I speak? His life was an anthem of praise to Christ; his life is the benediction that he has left us; and his character—we know that he was gentle and good; we know that he was true and strong; we know that we could always trust him with perfect confidence; we know that he was firm when firmness was needed, and tender when tenderness was required. We know that he was like a rock in the sea when truth was in peril, and yet we know how easily entreated he was, even, I would almost say, from his convictions, but I dare not—but always easily entreated when he could make peace to abide.

As to his work, I can only think of it as a finished temple, every seam pointed, the spire perfect and touching the sky, furnished to completeness, built on Christ, built of Christ, built for Christ.

Talk of death to-day! We are in the very midst of living things to-day. Ye are the temple that he built; your lives, into which he poured his own devoted life; your hearts, that he turned to Christ; your children, that he showed the way of righteousness; your homes, that will ever be sweet with the odor of his saintly life and his fervent prayers. And he found time to spare, even when so faithful to you that you could never complain; he found time, saved out of his own indulgence, to bless this city, to overflow himself upon the church that he loved, and to bring back the generous rewards that he so richly deserved. Intimacy alone can express it. Men or women who never were let into his inner soul cannot know him to-day. The closer the contact, the clearer the impression that he had sweet communions, and constant, with Christ.

I may be pardoned a single personal allusion, for doubtless it was this consideration that has made it my privilege to pay this word of tribute to Dr. Breed. Our congregations were very closely united, our communions were very sweet. We have spent days of prayer together; we have spent weeks of prayer together for the conversion of the world; we have often exchanged; we have had frequent communions, and I want to bear testimony to the constant friendliness. I want to bear testimony to the truth that never in all these years has there been seen above the surface, or an indication that there was beneath the surface, any bitterness or trouble, and I want to bear the testimony that this outward flow of fellowship and friendship had its counterpart in the closer relationships and fellowships of the pastors of these joint churches.

On Wednesday night, when we were compelled to give up hope, when the very disappointment made the departure seem the sadder, in order somehow to commune with the old friend for a little while, I took from the shelf the little book that I knew was fullest of himself, "Aboard and Abroad." It is more the reflection of the man than anything he ever wrote. It made conspicuous his convictions and his regard for righteousness, but it gave, what many of his works could never show, that outflow of his inner self that made fellowship so sweet.

In the first letter, that was written on shipboard, he calls to mind the harbor of the city that was familiar in his college days, and describes the receding harbor lights, and the crafts, great and small, passing by; he refers to the Statue, not complete, that was to guard the passage to the sea; he describes the lights of the city fading from view and the spires lost in the mists; you will remember how he closed that paragraph, "Out of the Narrows, out to the Sea," and as I laid down the book it seemed to me it was his own prophecy of to-day; it seemed to me that he had but anticipated the description of this longer journey that has left us sad upon the shore. It seemed to me I heard him calling back, "I have seen the city spires fade out of sight, I have seen the harbor lights grow dim, but I am out of the Narrows; I am out at Sea."

The Narrows look dark to us to-day, and deep, but he has passed the Narrows, and the Unknown Sea across which he floated seems to us lost in shadow and in mist.

But who ever taught us better than Dr. Breed to believe in the land that is beyond? Who ever taught us better than Dr. Breed to be sure that the Unknown Sea leads to the Father's house?

It was not a voyage, like the other, to a strange land. Dr. Breed is homeward bound to-day. Nay, home, for the vessel, doubtless, is already in her other harbor and the Master's welcome is received.

"Homeward bound." Let us not sorrow as those who have no hope. Many more have met him on the other shore than mourn for him here. Men and women whom he wrought with here; men and women for whom he opened the gate to the Father's house; the Master whom he served; more than crowd this house, are rejoicing to-day. Dr. Breed will betimes come back. Every time I feel a nobler impulse in the memory of his noble life, every time I am prompted to do better work in memory of his untiring zeal, every time I can hope that my character is lifted in the memory of his purity and faithfulness, I believe I will see his manly form, and that the sweet spirit will, through that sweet face, once more smile its benediction on my soul.

Whoever may occupy this pulpit, or whoever may uncover the symbols of the sacrament, as long as there remains a man, or woman, or child in these pews that ever heard his voice, that ever looked upon his face, so long will there be those to witness to his faithfulness. The work that he did, by the grace of God, will abide, his monument among us, and follow him, as his witness, to his eternal home of rest and reward.

MEMORIAL SERMON,

BY

REV. HENRY C. McCOOK, D.D.,

DELIVERED AT THE

WEST SPRUCE STREET PRESBYTERIAN CHURCH,

ON SABBATH MORNING APRIL, 21st, 1889.

WILLIAM PRATT BREED was born in Greenbush, New York, August 23d, A. D., 1816.

Modern science reaches across the interval of four thousand years to clasp hands with Moses at the Mount of Sinai in declaring the importance of heredity as a factor in the character and destiny of men. We cannot, therefore, pass unnoticed or unvalued the Providence that gave our friend a mental and physical temperament drawn from the sturdy blood which has done so much to make our country great. He could join with Cowper in that worthy pride which inspired the lines—

> " My boast is not that I deduce my birth
> From loins enthroned and rulers of the earth ;
> But higher far my proud pretensions rise—
> The son of parents passed into the skies."

On both sides, his ancestors were of old Puritan stock, and both paternal and maternal grandfathers were soldiers in the Revolutionary War. He would sometimes speak laughingly of the honor of which his family had been deprived by the historic inaccuracy which formed the battle of " Breed's Hill " into the battle of " Bunker Hill." On the father's side the line is traced back directly to Allen Breed, a wholesale grocer of Liverpool, who came over in the little fleet that carried Governor Winthrop and eight hundred immigrants from the old country to the new world in 1630. It was a thorough Puritan stock, with a strong strain of independence and dissent, that led a number of the descendants to branch off into the principles of the Baptists and the Society of Friends.

I.

A stirring incident of his babyhood, which involved great peril to his life, was a freshet in the Hudson River, which surrounded the house, threatening its destruction, flooded the lower story, and cut it off completely from the mainland. Fortunately, a sudden drop in the temperature froze thick the flooded stream, while it was yet above the first floor, and the parents escaped over the ice, carrying in their arms William and another child. Thus, of this babe, like Moses of old, it might be said that he was "saved from the waters."

In 1819 the family removed to Stamford, Connecticut; and in 1822 to New Hope, Pennsylvania, where the father had a bakery until his death in 1827.

The widowed mother and four dependent children were left with no legacy but their industry, sturdy independence and piety. With characteristic pluck and foresight, the widow removed to New York City,* as a more advantageous field in which to raise a family, as opportunities for employment were more numerous and remunerative than in a small country town. The metropolis of the Nation had long been Philadelphia, but New York had just begun that gigantic development which soon placed her beyond her ancient rival.

His Boyhood. Yet the city still bore many traces of its Dutch origin. Life was more simple. The conditions of society had not been revolutionized from their primitive American type by the influx of a dominant foreign element. There was, therefore, an incalculable difference between the environment of a lad of that period and of the boy who to-day is educated in our modern metropolis.

His education was chiefly under the influence of his widowed mother, a woman of strong character and earnest piety, whose faithful

---

* About 1829.

life, as with so many mothers, lives and forever shall live in the work of her son. At an early age he went to learn the bookbinder's trade, and in this occupation gained a sympathy with hand workers, with the lowly and the struggling, which never forsook him, even in his most prosperous days.

We have a glimpse of the lad, sitting or standing at his bench, sleeves tucked up, a huge workman's apron girt upon him, busy at the details of his craft, while spread before him on the bench was a book of Latin or mathematics. We recall the great men and women who have accomplished an education **Apprentice Life.** under like difficult circumstances. Vice-President Wilson with books upon the shoemaker's bench beside him; Elihu Burritt, the learned blacksmith, studying languages amidst the flying sparks of the red iron on the anvil; Livingstone, tutoring himself for his life work as missionary pioneer of the dark continent of Africa while he pushed the weaver's shuttle and conned the book that lay upon the loom; Roxanna Ward, the mother of Henry Ward Beecher, studying while she spun flax, tying her book to her distaff. We are apt to regard these as special cases, but the vision, which we have just recalled, of the New York bookbinder's 'prentice boy, permits us to believe that in our great Republic a multitude of youth have been and still are engaged in fitting themselves amid daily toils for higher and more useful positions. There is nothing more creditable in Dr. Breed's career than the manner in which he thus entered upon it, conning his lessons as he plied a mechanic's task. In the last year of his life his boyhood's training revived, and in an upper room of his house in Sixteenth Street he fitted up a little shop, and employed himself in rebinding some of his well worn library books.

During his apprenticeship occurred a fire that destroyed the establishment in which he wrought, and there survives a family story of the boy fleeing from the flames, through the streets, clad in his shop apron, breaking in upon his mother and crying, with that touch of humor so strongly developed in later years, " Well, ma, my tin cup is gone!"

II.

Dr. Breed was a child of the Church, and an example of the view that those who give the best service to Christ are commonly those who make the earliest consecration of their powers to Him. His pastor was Dr. Krebs of the Rutgers Street Church, of whom he always spoke with the greatest respect and in the tenderest terms, as one under whose ministry he had been led to Christ.

In his twenty-fifth anniversary address, he said: " It is not, by any means, a surprise to me to find the members of the church entertaining kindly feelings towards the pastor, because I have occupied the place of a member of a congregation myself, and have known what it was to have a pastor. In the home of my widowed mother, in New York, I knew very well, and all there knew very well, that if ever there was need of sympathy, if ever there was need of counsel, if ever there was need of service, there was one man on Manhattan Island who could be appealed to with a certainty of prompt and favorable response, our truly beloved pastor, Dr. John M. Krebs." *

Those of us who remember Dr. Krebs will recall a sturdy figure, somewhat inclined to stoutness, round cheeks, bushy eyebrows and hair, a genial, kindly look upon a face that had strong characteristics of the historic Dutch ancestry of New York, and a burly form, habitually clothed in a full dress suit.

One day our apprentice lad, then sixteen years old, was seen timidly passing through the streets of New York to the house of this pastor. It

---

* Quarter Century Anniversary, page 109.

was a heavy heart that he dragged up the "stoop," I have heard him say. But when he came out again, he did not stop to take the steps, but leaped from the door at one bound, ran away as fast as he could to tell his beloved mother the joyful tidings that the lost was found; that his soul was at peace, and that his life had been forever consecrated to Jesus!

He did not wait for a ministerial ordination to engage in the work of God. We behold him going up and down the streets of the city as a tract distributor. It was then, perhaps, a more popular business than now, although never was

First Christian Work.

there a period which furnished greater opportunities than the present day for the wise use of the printed page in disseminating the doctrines of salvation. That, at least, was Dr. Breed's view; and in subsequent life, as a member and long the honored President of the Presbyterian Board of Publication, he had opportunity to give a wide and practical scope to the experience and convictions born of that service.

For years the young convert engaged in this faithful duty, going from house to house, in the garrets, cellars, up lanes and alleys, seeing for himself the mass of neglected sin and misery that hovels itself in the hidden places of great cities, and gathered that experience and sympathy which made him in later days personally, and through the faithful missionary of his church, a friend and helper of the poor. This feature of his early life in New York City had a strange influence upon his destiny, and that of this congregation, which will presently appear.

He prepared for college under the tuition of Rev. Dr. John Owen, working at intervals as a journeyman bookbinder. His college training was received in the University of the City of New York.

III.

Mr. Breed began his theological studies at the Union Seminary, New York City, but after one year spent at that institution, he went to Princeton, where he graduated, A. D. 1847. There were giants in those days at this venerable seat of learning, as, indeed, there always have been; **Seminary Life.** and a walk through the Campo Santo of modern Presbyterianism, that simple but most famous Princeton burial ground, hard by College Campus and Seminary Hall, will reveal to the visitor, as he reads upon the marble such names as Hodge and Alexander and Miller, the intellectual, spiritual and theological furnishings that entered into the ministerial outfit of the young candidate. No wonder that under such influences he grew into a sturdy orthodoxy, and went forth to his work one of the best furnished of his class for the duties of the sacred office.

There is little variety in the ordinary life of the Seminarian, but one interesting episode marked young Breed's theological course. Just after receiving his licensure, he went South to spend a year in teaching at Montpelier Springs, near Savannah, Georgia, in order to secure funds to pay his way through the seminary. At that period it took a letter four weeks to go from Baltimore to Montpelier. There were no envelopes, no postage stamps, and the old-fashioned folded and sealed letters cost twenty-five cents apiece. Those were the days when slavery spread her dark pall above the Southland, and here the licentiate came in contact with an institution which in future days wrought the turmoils of the Rebellion, and which was only burned away from the nation's life by the fires of a civil war. If in after-years he was an enthusiastic patriot and an earnest anti-slavery man, it was because he knew by personal observation the evils of the institution.

During this service he was invited to supply the pulpit of a Protestant Episcopal Church in the neighborhood. He accepted the invitation, and, arrayed in the ordinary episcopal robes, read the services of that Church and preached his sermons, evidently to the entire satisfaction of all the community. What a curious and striking commentary upon the simpler and sweeter usages of that time! It would be well nigh impossible to conceive of such a thing occurring to-day in a congregation of that venerable communion ; and yet it gives us pleasure to believe that in such fellowship of Christian service the life of half a century ago lay nearer to the heart of Christ and the primitive usages, not only of the Apostolic Church, but of that Reformation in which the Anglican communion was born. Such a landmark as this incident permits us to see that in some respects our generation has retrograded rather than progressed.

An Episcopal rector, quoad sacra.

In the Seminary, a little band of students bound themselves together for prayer and conference upon the work of Foreign Missions, among whom Dr. Breed found a place. His interest in Foreign Missions was deep, and he was almost ready to offer himself to the Church for foreign service.*

One day a letter was placed in his hand by the venerable Dr. Archibald Alexander. It was written by Dr. Charles C. Beatty, of Steubenville, Ohio, and it asked that one of the students then about to be graduated be invited to visit Steubenville with a view of settlement over the Second Presbyterian Church of that place. The letter was unexpected, and dropped into young Breed's hands as from the very clouds. He decided to visit the church and take a look at the field, and the result was a call and decision to accept. He returned east, married (September, 1847) and took back to his western home as a bride the woman who for all the years of his long life remained at his side the happy, beloved, and helpful companion of his trials, his toils and his triumphs.

First Call.

---

* Historical Discourse, page 60.

3

In going to Ohio the young couple traveled six days, three of which were spent in canal boats. That simple fact startles one with the image of the wonderful progress which our country has made in the last generation.

IV.

The field to which the new minister had come was at that time one of remarkable interest. The city, which bears the name of a distinguished soldier of the Revolution, one of the founders of the Society of the Cincinnati, is situated on the north bank of the Ohio river, just beyond the Pennsylvania line. The principal part of the town is built upon a semi-circular, alluvial flat that reaches from the river's front to a high wall of hills, up whose slopes the suburbs of the city have gradually climbed. On the opposite bank of the river, stretching up between the Ohio and Pennsylvania borders, is what was then known as the Pan Handle of Virginia; slave territory it was in those ante-bellum days, before the State of West Virginia had been cut from the western flank of the Old Dominion.

Physical Environments.

Opposite the upper portion of the city, on the Virginia side, was a beautiful little valley known as the Cove, that broke the line of the cliffs and added to the charm of the scenery. From these hills of Steubenville, Thomas Cole, the famous pioneer of American landscape painting (as I have been told by my mother, who was one of his pupils), made his studies of the scenery which he wrought into his four celebrated paintings known as the Voyage of Life.

Steubenville, O.

In this beautiful site a vigorous population had settled. Three confluent tides of migration were flowing during the early part of this century into Ohio, which was then the gateway of the West. One tide came from New England, chiefly the State of Connecticut, swept across northern New York, carrying with it some of the assimilated population of that section, and occupied the northwestern corner of Ohio, known as the "Connecticut or Western Reserve." This was the home of Joshua Giddings, Bluff Ben. Wade and President Garfield. Another stream, following a little lower parallel, came from the State of Pennsylvania, chiefly from the beautiful central valleys among the Allegheny mountains. But the pioneers were the Scotch and Scotch-Irish population from the rugged foot-hills of the Alleghenies and the green wheat fields of Washington county, who crossed the Ohio border into the new State. There came with them, though not of them as yet, numerous colonies from the Pennsylvania Germans, who carried into their new home, Stark, Columbiana and Jefferson counties, their thrifty German ways and the bright red barns, such as one still sees gleaming amidst the golden fields of Lancaster.

From the border States of the South a Southern migratory wave was flowing northward, some of whom found place along the Ohio River as far up as Steubenville. Representatives of all these and other incoming populations were found in that city. No wonder that Ohio is famous as a land within which mighty men were born, and cultured and prepared for the great work **Parish Population.** which God had given them to do in this Republic! Small praise is that to Ohio herself, for it was the best blood and brain, vigor and brawn of the Eastern States that had come to mingle their energy with their blood upon the new soil, and make it thus a mighty Commonwealth.

I recall among the men of influence in Steubenville of that day such names as that of Senator Tappan, Edwin M. Stanton, the great War Secretary, and his partner, Colonel George W. McCook; Daniel V. Collier, Colonel James Collier, General Stokley; the warm-hearted Kentuckian, Dr. Comingo, my own beloved pastor; the Moodys, McDowells, Sherrards, Kilgores, Conns, Leavitts, Means, Andrews, Morse, Leavitt, Dike, Spencer, and a host of others, all of them men of mark, or men of high metal.

The old First Church, under the pastorate of Dr. Comingo was full, and Dr. Beatty, the principal of the Female Seminary, was the chief mover in establishing a second congregation. A house of worship had been built in a part of the city well removed from the mother church, and a flourishing congregation had already been gathered into it. This church, though known on the Presbyterian records and in legal documents as the Second Church, was popularly known, at least among the young men of the city, as the "Seminary Church." Here the young women of Beatty's Seminary worshipped; and it was **Beatty's Female Seminary.** one of the sights of the town to behold the long column of bright young women marching two-and-two, on a Sunday morning, to the Church. The chancel seats on either side of the pulpit were filled by them, and they overflowed into the front pews on either side. At that period this school was perhaps the leading one in the West and Southwest. Up the Ohio River, in the steamboats or "packets" that then walked the waters of our Western rivers, and all along the Mississippi and its branches, came from the plantations of the South young women to receive their education. From the far West and Northwest just then opening; from the Eastern counties of Ohio, and all the region around about Pittsburgh, possessed by a sturdy Presbyterian population, the best of the land were garnered to this seat of education.

It was no small task to preach to such a company, to say nothing of the numbers of cultivated people who occupied the pews beyond the chancel. It must have been an especially embarrassing position for a young man. Here Dr. Breed took up his profession and began his life work. That it was a successful ministry the records of **Fruits of First Ministry.** the Assembly abundantly show. After a year, gracious clouds of blessing gathered over the congregation, and God set before Mr. Breed that precious luxury, the young pastor's first revival. It was a heavenly shower, and from that time at intervals other like showers fell. During the eight years of his ministry, Dr. Breed received to the communion 382 souls, 254 of them on confession of faith.* Certainly this is a remarkable record, an average of 32 conversions a year!

I have alluded to the Female Seminary feature of that pastorate, not simply with the view of giving you a picture of the young man's surroundings, but because it formed a most important factor in his usefulness. Among those young ladies occurred a large proportion of these conversions. The Seminary was a most useful field, and those bright young spirits, there consecrated to God, went back to their homes to exercise an influence that can never be fully weighed until the Day of Judgment. They became the wives, many of them, of distinguished men of the already established or soon to be established States. They are found today occupying positions of honor in high places, among the notables of our country. Many have been the faithful wives of faithful ministers; and greater honor still, not a few of them have found congenial service and a grave in missionary service on foreign fields.

V.

Dr. Breed's preaching, as I remember it, was at that period not greatly different in style from that which is so well known by this congregation, except that it was perhaps a little more florid. He was called "a flowery preacher." This phrase in that section and period did not carry the meaning which we would give it. The prevailing tone of preaching was severely theological, didactic, inornate almost to barrenness, logical, formal, punctilious in divisions and subdivisions, lacking in the emotional, a faculty which was remanded to the

As a Preacher.

* Historical Discourse, p. 17.

Methodists, most fortunately for that noble communion, and often was unduly prolonged. In some of the congregations the old-fashioned hour-glass still held its place upon the pulpit.

I remember my boyhood's pastor, in a neighboring Ohio town, turning the glass when he rose to preach, preaching until the sand had all run out, and occasionally reversing the glass again as he passed into his "finally." I remember, too, on one rare occasion when the sermon ceased ere the hour's sand had run, that an elder greeted the pastor after service with a somewhat dolorous and rebuking tone, sweetened by the rich Doric accent of North Ireland: "Ah, docthor, you gev us scant measure, the daay!" I cannot say that I endorsed the elder's opinion, and there was a growing class of dissenters on that point. It was the older and conservative element that called Mr. Breed a "flowery preacher," and the dissenters approved the style, whatever the name implied. In fact, the young pastor of the Second Church had simply dropped into the current of the age and went with the stream just far and fast enough to do good service as one of Christ's fishers of men, casting the Gospel net into it by the way. His sermons blossomed with the beauty of that Nature which he loved so well, and he delighted to ornament them with quotations from the varied fields of literature, science and history. He was a popular preacher, not only in his own congregation, and among the young particularly, for whom he had strong attractions, but throughout the city and surrounding country. At the meetings of Presbytery and Synod, there was no one whom the people more willingly heard, and when it was known that Dr. Breed would preach, he was sure to have a full congregation. But the chief power of his preaching lay in the pure, sweet, simple but strong and faithful presentation of the very "marrow of divinity," the evangelical doctrine of salvation by grace through Jesus Christ alone.

The account of Dr. Breed's pulpit qualities would be incomplete without reference to his work among children and youth. He had a happy facility in addressing young people, which, in the days of his early ministry, was as rare as delightful. He was in the van of that great army that in these days is covering the world of child-life with sweet, simple, appropriate and helpful effort. **Work among Children.** The best picture of Dr. Breed's power and methods in this field that I can give, is presented in the following letter from a well-known Philadelphia pastor, Dr. John Henry Sharpe, who was a lad in Dr. Breed's first Sunday School. He thus writes :—

" There comes up before me, most vividly, a recollection of my youthful days in dear old Steubenville. It was on the Fourth of July, and probably in the year 1854 or '55. We celebrated the day in the Second Church by taking a Sunday-school excursion down the Ohio, many members of the congregation also going along. To my youthful impressions of the occasion there was a great company on board, and Dr. Breed was the life of it all. Our excursion carried us as far as the little town of Warrenton, Ohio, below Wellsburgh, where we landed. Not long afterward we formed a procession and marched up through the village to one of its churches. I presume there had been some arrangement beforehand for the exercises that followed. The only fact that I remember with distinctness is that Mr. Breed, then and there, gave a Fourth of July address, whose main points have ever since dwelt vividly in my memory.

" It consisted of two stories of boys, whose names he strictly withheld until the denouement in each case. The first was the story of a boy who loved the sea, and whose heart and imagination were fired by what he saw of the men-of-war riding up and down the bay before his widowed mother's home, and of the soldiers and sailors who were frequently visitors at the homestead of his elder brother with whom he lived. At last a commission to be midshipman was procured for him, and the evening of the day before which he was to go on board and sail away on the high seas arrived. Then followed the scene of a mother in tears going to say farewell to her boy, and breaking down ; and then the affectionate son so touched that, though it cost him the dream of his life to that hour, he decided he would not leave his mother, and cast up his commission. The vessel waited for him next morning, and when he did not come it sailed away without him.

" ' Who was that boy ? ' When Mr. Breed asked that question, I do not know whether I knew the answer or not, but I know that he had wound us up to such a pitch that there was a great shout—' George Washington ! '

" As soon as the excitement had subsided somewhat Mr. Breed had launched out upon another story. This was of another boy, whose mother, if I recollect the story aright, was also a widow. But the boy was a totally different one. He was disobedient and cruel. He robbed birds' nests. He broke glass bottles into small pieces and scattered them where barefooted little children would tread on them and cut their feet. This boy too lived near the sea, and he wanted to become a sailor, but his mother would not hear to it. But despite his mother's tears and fears, at last he got all things in readiness one night, and then ran off and enlisted in a ship, leaving his mother to mourn his unknown fate. This story the speaker further touched up as to the after history of the boy, and the climax came with the demand for his name. Again came a thundering answer, but I must confess that I was not then enough of a historian to join in naming the traitor, ' Benedict Arnold ! '

" I have never since then, I believe, heard these two opposite and contrasting histories. They were wonderfully effective, and they illustrate a power, which I believe that Dr. Breed possessed in an unique degree, of impressing the youthful mind with telling facts, sentiments and lessons.

" I believe I mentioned to you the other day his summer visit to Steubenville in 1858, when he accompanied the Sunday School on an excursion up the river to the "Half Moon Farm." On that occasion he was obliged to address us, and standing up there in the woods with a leaf in his hand, he discoursed about the myriads of living things in every green leaf and in every drop of water. It was a startling revelation to me, and doubtless it was to others. I cannot but believe that it was his wonderful skill in gaining and holding the youthful attention by his vivid power of picturesque description that made his story of the infusoria and animalcula of nature so fascinating and ineffacable.

A Nature Talk.

"Let me refer to still another delightful memory of mine. I was a scholar in the Infant School taught by Mrs. Breed. As the holidays drew on I was confined at home by illness of some sort. Dr. and Mrs. Breed sent out invitations to the pupils of the Infant School to come to a New Year's party at the parsonage. I remember my fear that I should not be well enough to be allowed to go. But go I did, and such an evening we had! First, we assembled in the parlor. We had many gleesome games there, Mr. Breed joining in them as if he were truly one of our number. I remember quite well how when we were all ranged in rows close to the wall, all around the room, and sitting on the floor, he passed around and swept his two hands through my two palms held close together, in the game, 'Buttoner! Buttoner! Who has the button?' I did not get the button nor do I know now who did, but his merry eyes and the touch of his hand are before me now as they were then. Later on we were led mysteriously up stairs. The room was darkened and we were cautioned not to be frightened, but to look intently at the wall opposite. Suddenly a great open-mouthed, glaring-eyed tiger leaped out in a circle of light. It was the first in a series of magic lantern pictures with which he entertained us in a way we could not fail to remember all our lives long."

A Night at the Manse.

Dr. Breed was equally effective as a pastor. During those eight years of ministry, the first years, be it remembered, of his public life, not a jar of discord was ever heard within the congregational bounds. A single exception, perhaps, should be allowed. It occurred upon the introduction of an organ as an aid to congregational praise. People of our generation and our present surroundings cannot appreciate the strong feelings and convictions which some of the worthy fathers and mothers, from

As a Pastor. Scotland and Northern Ireland especially, entertained concerning instrumental aid in the musical parts of worship. To them the "Kist o' whustles," as they contemptuously denominated the organ, was only "an abomination" in the house of the Lord. On the day when such an instrument was introduced into the Second Church of Steubenville, at the first sound of the organ, a most excellent and venerable lady, with the true Caledonian blue running current through her veins, started from her seat, and stood stalwart, upright in her pew. She acted as if a thunderbolt had suddenly fallen upon the church. Turning toward the organ loft, she listened a moment, as though to assure herself that the abomination had actually invaded the sanctuary; then with a frown overspreading her face, with head erect, with lips firmly set, she stalked down the aisle, and left the church, never again to grace with her presence that "desecrated spot."

VI.

Into this field of peaceful usefulness came an agent of that Eastern invasion which has so often raided the pulpits of the west. That agent was Mr. Morris Patterson, a name forever honored and remembered in this sanctuary. He appeared as commissioner from the congregation of West Spruce Street Church. On the 4th, of April, 1856, the Presbytery of Philadelphia had met; a call was presented for the services of William Pratt Breed, and the congregation obtained leave to prosecute the same before the Presbytery of Steubenville. I have always understood that the direct instrumentality in this call was the late Daniel L. Collier, Esq., who had removed from Steubenville to Philadelphia, to whose worthy and highly respectable citizens he soon showed what sort of material could be provided from the banks of the Ohio. Knowing as he did the young pastor of the Second congregation, he discerned in him the qualities that would make the newly organized West Spruce Street Church a success, and upon his recommendation the matter was investigated, with the results announced.

Call to West Spruce Street.

In the meantime great was the perturbation of spirit in that beautiful amphitheatre on the western shore of the Ohio. The centre of perturbation was the parsonage of the Second Presbyterian Church, from which it overflowed into and through the congregation.*

The Philadelphia call was resisted by the people of Steubenville, led by Dr. Beatty, who felt most keenly, perhaps, the loss that threatened him and his pupils. The Presbytery of Steubenville almost unanimously advised Mr. Breed to remain upon his field.

But Dr. Boardman and the newly organized West Spruce Street Church were the sort of Presbyterians who believed in grit as well as grace; and having once entertained the idea that Dr. Breed was their appointed pastor, they could not forego the conviction that whatsoever was foreordained *must* come to pass! They, therefore, came before the Presbytery of Philadelphia and upon their action, that venerable body authorized them again to prosecute their call. The result is thus recorded by Dr. Breed in his diary, which it appears he was in the habit of keeping during the most of his life. Unhappily, that diary has been lost, or at least has not been accessible for the preparation of this memorial discourse. " April

Presbyterial Conflict.

---

* Historical Discourse, p. 16.

7th, 1856. A most trying day. Presbytery dissolved the pastoral relation between me and the Second Church of Steubenville. Having been led along step by step, I seem to see that I must go to the West Spruce Street Church in Philadelphia, but Presbytery having once refused, was still wavering, was divided, and I having decided the matter in my own mind, let them know fully and plainly how I felt, and they acted at last with no great lack of unanimity. It is painful, but if it prove happy for this Church and for that, I shall never recall the pain with any regret. May the good Spirit of God send his smile upon all concerned."*

How strange and recondite are the influences that draw our lives in this way or that, and bind the hearts of men together or force them asunder! Who would have thought that the links of the chain of Providence that drew the Steubenville pastor to his Philadelphia home, had been wrought upon the anvil of Providence in the days when the young bookbinder and college student was serving God as a tract distributor in New York City? Who would have thought that the decision which changed a life, which moulded the destiny of a great congregation, which has made the future for an unknown number of souls, was all based upon a blunder? Yet so it was.

Dr. Breed has left the facts on record and we cannot be in doubt. He always had dread of rather than desire for a luxurious pastorate. He never had conceived the ambition to occupy what is called a "leading church." His work among the poor of New York City, his profound sympathy with their interests, and conviction that nothing but Christ and his salvation would bring relief and genuine healing to all their burdens and woes, had deeply impressed his mind. He never forgot the experiences of those days. And whenever in his Steubenville work the thought was suggested by letters from abroad as to the advantage of another field of labor, the reply to himself was, " No ; if ever I leave this field volun-

---

* Historical Discourse, p. 19.

tarily, it will be to go to some great city and labor among the poor." Filled with this purpose and spirit he arrived in Philadelphia. The Church to which he was called he knew to be a colony from the Tenth Church, and the conclusion which he had formed, and which, reasoning from his New York experience, he thought at the time a natural one, was that it was a sort of Church mission enterprise. Among the first questions that he asked Dr. Boardman, in correspondence, was, " Will the labors there be among the poor?" Dr. Boardman simply answered, " The rich and the poor meet together."

Judge, then, of his emotions, of his profound surprise and, as he declares, disappointment, when he stood at the corner of Seventeenth and Spruce streets, amid the rubbish and débris of the then uncompleted but splendid sanctuary, and, among the homes of those who were to be his people and associates, beheld how **A Strange Mistake.** different was the realization from the expectation! This was no mission chapel! This was no missionary enterprise, in the sense, at least, of labor among the lowly poor! What were his sentiments under the circumstances? We know, for he has written them : " When I reached Philadelphia and saw the field to which I had come, I exclaimed, ' Well, man proposes; God disposes. But here I am, and now to the work that lies before me."* Thus, like a good Christian and good Calvinist as he was, he accepted the fact of a leading Providence, and beholding the way of God walked therein.

Though not precisely in the way that he anticipated, his expectations were not disappointed; for, after twenty-five years of service, he could testify to his own conscience and to his God that, although few pastoral fields include homes of wealth fuller of all that can delight a pastor's heart than the charge to which he had come, yet he found in them a ready response to his appeals in behalf of less fortunate brethren, and

* Historical Discourse.

was enabled, through the agency of others, to bear the Gospel of Christ to a multitude of the poor. Perhaps he thus accomplished the worthy purpose which had been a moving motive in sundering the Ohio pastoral relation, even more fully than in any other way.

The lecture room of the new church was opened for worship on Sabbath, May 18th, 1856, and on June 4th following, at the Tenth Church,

Installation. the installation of the pastor-elect took place. For some time thereafter the two pastors, Dr. Boardman and Mr. Breed, preached alternately in the mother church and the church on Spruce street. In fact, it was a collegiate congregation, but this arrangement was not of long duration. Collegiate churches and dependent colonies have never been popular in Philadelphia. The genius of the people tends too strongly to independence, and the sturdy American character of its population chafes under the idea of dependence upon another church.

Next to a man's own congregation, nothing probably has a greater influence upon his character and ministry than the character of his

Ministerial Environment. neighbors and associates in ministerial life. The first experience of our western brother was gained at his admission to Presbytery. He had been ordained by the Steubenville Presbytery, and a more truly orthodox "Old School" body, to say the least, nowhere could be found, as I can well attest, having been ordained by the same venerable body. Coming from this Presbytery after an eight years' pastorate, it might well have produced something of a surprise to know that the Philadelphia brethren insisted upon putting the applicant for membership through the same catechetical exercises required of an incoming licentiate. But those were days when the spirit of "Old School" and "New School" was still rampant in the land. Jealousy, watchfulness, and alas! too often bitterness, if not bigotry, marked the relations of ministers and elders with their co-presbyters. Therefore, the venerable Dr. McDowell was put to the front and, with Dr. Musgrave in the chair, whose proclivities were, to say the least, not very strongly towards moderation, we may be well assured that Mr. Breed, of Ohio, was thoroughly tested as to his soundness in the faith, before his papers were passed upon and he greeted with the right hand of fellowship. He stood the catechism not only with success theologically, but with profound good temper, not without a mirthful glance at the seeming oddity, not to say absurdity, of the scene.

Go back to the days of 1856, and call the roll of the men who then stood foremost in the Presbyterian pulpits of Philadelphia, There was Albert Barnes, *facile princeps*, massive as a mountain, firm as a mountain's granite heart, pure as the crystal streamlet that trickles down the mountain's side; a character guileless and sweet as the wood-

Albert Barnes.

flowers that bloom in the mountain dells, and living a life as fertile to the world as the plains that skirt the mountain foot rich with the fretting of winter's frosts and sweepings of summer rains. He held his place in the First Church, the mother of us all, in the midst of a people one of whose noblest characteristics has always been unswerving loyalty to their pastors. Close by, in the old Pine Street Church, which the soldiers of King George converted into a stable during the Revolutionary days, as a testimony of the feelings with which they regarded the "pestilent Presbyterians," was Dr. Brainard, strong, evangelical, masterful, beloved, as ready for a revival or a patriotic meeting as for a horseback ride along the country roads and under the branching trees of Hamiltonville, just beyond the Schuylkill.

The cultured and classical Shields was in the old Second Church, which has since crossed the Presbytery borders and built it a sanctuary on Walnut street. Dr. Cheeseman was in the Fourth Church, in those days, or a little earlier at least, somewhat profanely denominated among certain of its enemies as the "old fourth-proof Church." At the Arch Street Church crowds of people thronged to hear Dr. Charles Wadsworth, prince of sermonizers, most awkward of orators with his one circulatory gesture, yet most attractive of preachers, eloquent in diction, glowing with evangelical zeal, and all abloom with figures drawn from every field of thought. Alexander Macklin had, for his thoroughly Scottish name, a most harmonious setting in the historic Scots Church, which has at last renewed its youth and found lodgment on South Broad street. Butler, in West Philadelphia, a rural part of the city in those days, was laying the foundations of the Walnut Street Church, which stands to-day easily in the forefront of our best congregations. The Central Church, which has since, like many others, been put on wheels and carried up to Broad and Fairmount Avenue, was under the ministry of the eloquent Henry Steele Clark.

Johnstone "of that ilk," as he was proud to characterize himself, with a glance at his good Scotch ancestors, was up in Kensington. He ruled his congregation well,—*ruled* it, for, in the admiring language of one of his devoted parishioners, " he was a lordly mon." With a warm heart in his big chest, and a laughing eye in his rosy face; with hands as quick to generous deeds as was his tongue to fiery speech, he well illustrated the motto of his beloved Irish Church, " Ardens sed virens." At the Sixth Church, down on Spruce street, was the gentle and courtly Dr. Jones, soon to pass into the Secretaryship of the Board of Ministerial Relief. Dr. E. P. Rodgers, not yet transferred to the Dutch Collegiate Church of New York, was drawing crowds to Penn Square, and waging unremitting conflict within himself between his love for fine pictures and the limitations of his salary. How they would wonder, these last two, could they wake from their long sleep and walk out Chestnut street to Thirty-seventh and see the stalwart child of the happy union between the old Sixth and Seventh Churches—our present "Tabernacle."

In the Clinton Street Church was Henry S. Darling, loving, beloved, formal but friendly and sympathetic, the beau ideal of a clergyman, not only in his mental furnishings, but in his outward deportment. Up in the Northern Liberties Dr. Thomas J. Shepperd wielded his bishop's crook with dignity and power. The venerable Dr. John McDowell was bringing forth fruit in old age in the Spring Garden Church, little dreaming of the days to come when the garden walls which he builded and guarded with such orthodox watchfulness should be invaded by a Unitarian from far-away Armenia. Robert Watts at Westminster was displaying qualities which soon won for him a call to an honored professorship in the Belfast School of the Prophets. Dr. John Jenkins, rich in his pulpit endowments, but too English in sentiment for the coming days of civil war, was in Calvary Church, the nearest neighbor and the powerful New School rival of West Spruce Street Church. Calvary was vigorous with new blood, and, virile with the consecrated wealth of men like Baldwin and Baird, sent forth such ecclesiastical children as Tabor, Olivet and Hope. In the Tenth Church, at Twelfth and Walnut, was Dr. Henry A. Boardman, whose master hand had carved and framed the enterprise materialized at last in the West Spruce colony, to which Dr. Breed was called.

Henry A. Boardman.

There were few congregations in those days, there have been few in any day, that in personnel could be held the peers of the people to whom he preached; and the man was worthy of such a flock. His was the Damascus blade, keen, polished, wielded by one of the best trained and fairest poised minds that the Church has ever known.

Musgrave, too, was here, Moderator of the Presbytery, his "thunder hammer of Thor" in every way in sharp contrast with the polished weapon which Boardman wielded. There

Dr. Musgrave.

was no sight in Presbytery better worth seeing than a conflict of courteous debate between these two great leaders, so strangely unlike each other in nearly all their characteristics, yet thoroughly united on some of the greatest movements of the Church. Up in the Logan Square Church was Dr. John Patton. Where is the Logan Square Church? History moves so swiftly, and the changes in a great city are so many that the names familiar a quarter of a century ago become obliterated.

4

That Church has disappeared from our rolls, but Dr. Patton still is among us, not as an active pastor, indeed, but his well-known face is yet familiar in ministerial associations. Of all the company whose names have been mentioned, he and only one other remain. The affable and erudite Dr. Blackwood of the Ninth Church is the single pastor within our city limits that greeted Dr. Breed at his coming.

VII.

How impossible by simple arithmetic to sum up such a ministry as Dr. Breed's. But figures have their value, and at least give an accepted standard of success. During the first twenty-five years of his ministry in Philadelphia 548 persons united with his Church on profession of their faith, an average of twenty-two conversions a year. About the same number were received upon certificate. How many others have been brought to Christ through this faithful man's ministry none but God can know. Certain it is that the saving influences of any minister in a large city Church are never to be measured by the results shown upon the records of his own Church membership.

Philadelphia Ministry.

Oftentimes the most fruitful part of a ministry for Christ is that which meets "strangers within the gates" and those who listen to the word in the frequent services wrought in other congregations, and in general public work. But taking the bare statistics of the two Churches which he served, it is a noble record—930 conversions. The number received during the interval from his quarter century celebration to his retirement from the active pastorate must have swollen this number to more than 1000 souls. A whole regiment of the Redeemed! What a noble army is that to march before the presence of the Throne in the day of final glory, and lay down their crowns at the feet of the Lamb, rejoicing in that salvation which was brought to them through the instrumentality of this faithful man of God.

Dr. Breed's new work was begun under many happy auspices, but scarcely was it under full way before it was met by the terrible financial crisis of 1857. As he expressed it, " This wild gale met our bark as she went out of port, straining her timbers, tearing her sails, but her flag brave hands had nailed to the mast." This crisis was followed by the great revival of '57 and '58, in which the new pastor took an earnest part, and which brought renewed strength to his congregation. To quote again his language, " When the pinnacles of our Zion began to glimmer with the rays of the morning, they were first swept by the financial tempest, and then gilded by the great religious awakening." *

The influence of this awakening upon Dr. Breed and his congregation extended through all his ministerial life. What a season it was ! The recollection thereof has not yet died from the memories of many living. On the 3d of February, 1858, began those Union Prayer Meetings in this city which afterward acquired so wide a notoriety. They were established on the pattern of the Fulton Street Prayer Meeting of New York, which had been started on the 23d of April preceding. The Philadelphia meeting began in an ante-room of what was then known as Jayne's Hall. For some days only twenty, forty and sixty persons attended. Suddenly the number went up to three hundred, and it was resolved, not without trepidation, to hold the next meeting in the large hall. The hall with seats for 2500 people was filled. The next day the curtain was drawn away from the stage, and it and the galleries were filled. The next day the partition between the smaller and larger room was taken down, and

Revival of '57-'58.

---

* Historical Discourse, p. 38.

the hall, from street to street, thrown open. " The meeting was unparalleled in the history of any city in any age. Wave after wave poured in from the closet, from the family, from the Church, until the great tidal wave rolled its mighty surge, swallowing up for the time all separate sects, creeds, denominations in the one great, glorious, only Church of the Holy Ghost." * The wave spread from one end of the Republic to the other, and its holy influences swept forward to the very beginning of that colossal struggle between the two sections of the country that began when the Sumter fires were kindled in '61. Indeed, it has been universally regarded as God's gracious preparation of his Church for the trials and temptations of that fratricidal war.

In its essential characteristics, Dr. Breed displayed in his Philadelphia bishopric the same qualities as preacher and pastor that marked his Ohio ministry. Advancing years, widened experiences and views of men and life, enlarged responsibilities and changed environments had, of course, their modifying influence; but there was no great revolution in style, no upheaval of nature, no birth of latent powers and faculties, no deliberate entrance upon a new manner of preaching and an antipodal career, as has sometimes occurred to ministers after such translation of labors. His life flowed on over the already well worn channel, broadened, fulled, diversified, but the same. One of his faithful elders thus describes it : " The gospel he has proclaimed has been no new-fangled invention of his own or of any other human brain. It has been ' the old, old story of Jesus and His love.'

Philadelphia Preaching.

"Sabbath after Sabbath, Wednesday after Wednesday, Friday after Friday, in season and out of season, has he come to us in the fulness of the preparation of the Gospel of peace ; and while he has held fast to the old landmarks, and stood firm upon the fundamental principles of truth as

* See Historical Discourse, p. 27.

the Presbyterian Church understands them, yet he has ever kept fully abreast with all the recent investigations of science and all its discoveries. He has been and is familiar with every art of modern infidelity, and has championed the truth against all the assaults of recent atheism, deism, evolution and **George Junkin's Estimate.** other kindred errors. History has yielded to him its treasures, Art has been his spoil, Literature has paid him tribute, and to-day his panoply for service in the Christian warfare is as complete as that of any of whom we have knowledge." *

Perhaps Dr. Breed's greatest power for service lay in the quality of his pastoral work. Just after his death I heard a little circle of ministers discussing his character and career. Several expressed the opinion that he owed very much of his success to his eldership and official members, men of strong individuality and sterling **Pastoral Work.** worth, whose moulding hands upon their pastor had shaped as well as sustained him. Certainly there is much to justify such a view, and no one more fully than Dr. Breed himself admitted it and expressed his obligations to his faithful friends. But there was one, at least, in that little circle, who had read more closely and more truthfully the facts which the testimony of these men reveals. Dr. Breed was the bishop *over* his flock. Power is not always noisy. Bluster is not force. The shoot of Niagara's current just above the Falls is as silent as the movement of the night stars. The babbling mountain brook makes far more noise. A growing corn-field on the fat prairies of Illinois cracks and snaps under the hot suns of August. But under the same vital force the forests of the Alleghenies are lifted up into mighty trunks, noiselessly as a sun-rising. Dr. Breed's power wrought silently, but it was none the less effective for that. This is the testimony of one of his noblest supporters,

---

* Mr. George Junkin's Address at Quarter-Centennial.

54

whose free-hearted help was one of the largest factors in his church's growth, Gustavus F. Benson.*

"That which impresses us in all this," he said, "is the fact that there must be some moving principle in it all, that there must be something not apparent which has stirred up these people, as with one heart, to come forward and show their affection for their pastor. Himself of a loving and sympathetic nature, the most ardent desire

Gustavus F. Benson's Testimony. of his soul to have souls, he has brought into this church, since he has been the pastor of it, some six hundred people, whose conversion under God has been brought about through his instrumentality. *His example has made this a working church.* The names of those of its members who have worked the hardest in their own Church, appear upon the rolls of managers of our benevolent societies, of our hospitals, of the boards of our Church. Indeed, I might almost say that wherever in this city good works are to be done, there you will find the names of the members of this Church.

"*He has made this people a liberal people.* It is said of the celebrated Dr. Adam Clark, the great Methodist commentator, one of the most learned men of his day, that when one of his congregation came to his study and told him with great glee that a certain man, noted alike for his wealth and his parsimony, had been converted, the Doctor very quietly turned around and asked, 'Have you converted his purse?' Our pastor is one of whom I may safely say that, in making conversions of his people, he has converted their purses. No Church other than this responds more quickly to any appeal that is made to them for benevolent or religious purposes; and the records of the general Assembly will show that in point of liberality, considered with respect to its proportionate size and wealth, this Church has not been behind any of our sister churches.

* Remarks at the Quarter-Century Celebration.

"*He has made this a loving Church.* Perhaps, in a larger degree than is generally the case in a city Church, this Church is like one great Christian family. The attachment of its people to their Church and to their pastor is so pronounced as to be remarkable ; and I was never more impressed with this fact than when, in the preparations for what I may call this family celebration, the entire unanimity and enthusiasm of the Church gave evidence of the love of its people for their pastor and of their love for one another."

Hear the testimony of another ruling elder, happily still among you, who also spoke on that occasion, Mr. George Junkin. "In one respect our history has been most remarkable. In our Session, our Board of Deacons, our Board of Trustees, our Congregational Meetings, our Bible Classes, our Dorcas Society, our Missionary Society, our Sabbath-school, our Sabbath-school Association, our Sewing School, our Choir (and it has always been a voluntary one), and in our whole congregation, we have never had a division, a quarrel, a discord, a strife, a scandal, a divided vote, a sense of alienation ! The current of our whole life has flowed on like a river, unbroken by a storm, and unchecked by an obstruction.

"And to what shall we attribute this blessed experience ? Not to us, who have composed this Church, in the various departments of Church work and organization to which I have alluded. The weaknesses of poor human nature have existed among us, just as everywhere ; and some of us are about as good specimens of crooked humanity as exist !

Mr. Junkin's Testimony.

"Why, then, this blessed experience of unbroken harmony ? I will tell you. Under God, it is due to him to whom the Prince of Peace, from the first, committed the care of this flock. His lovely, unselfish, self-sacrificing, tender, Christly spirit, with its indescribable, yet subtile and controlling influence, has pervaded all this people. Unconsciously to ourselves his has been the almost unseen and unnoticed hand which, with its magic and unfelt power, has guided all these elements of our natures, so that the entire Psalm of Life which this congregation has been singing down these years has been a harmony, and not a crashing discord. In all the qualities that constitute a faithful shepherd and bishop of the flock of Christ, our pastor, the Rev. William Pratt Breed, if not peerless, is the peer of any and all; and he has done his whole duty to the charge committed to his care."

As an illustration of Dr. Breed's wise and spiritual methods of administering his holy office, one incident may be referred to. At the communion of December, 1869, but one person appeared upon profession of faith. That seeming barrenness called for heart-searching and special prayer. The communion had

A Church Revival.

been preceded by a prayer-meeting in the Session room, which was full of solemnity, and in which impressions were made that afterwards ripened into hopeful conversions. Several cases of sickness and death followed quickly, touching at least three of the ruling elders of the Church. Nothing is more valuable to a pastor in winning souls for Christ than that antennal power which enables him to feel in the atmosphere pervading his congregation the presence of a spiritual awakening. No man can possess this who is not himself in close fellowship with the Eternal. Dr. Breed, with his keen spiritual power, discerned hopeful signs of a new religious life. His ear lay so close to the hearts of his people and to the face of his God that he could "hear the sound of a going in the tops of the trees." He called the people together and arranged for a series of meetings, beginning February 21st.

I remember those meetings well, for I had just come from St. Louis to enter upon my labors in this Eastern city. My experience of methods was so different from those which I found prevailing here, that I could not but watch with careful eye the methods of my new associates. It was a new thing to me to see a protracted meeting conducted by calling a different minister to

Revival Meeting Methods.

preach every night. In the West, when we were not compelled to do all such work ourselves, we depended upon the aid of one brother alone. This kaleidoscopic evangelizing was a great novelty. I wondered how it could succeed. It was my conviction that there was great loss in the introduction of new personalities, new voices, new modes of thinking and applying truth, new spiritual temperaments and temperature; that curiosity in the recurring sermons and divided interest in individuals would mar the success of the work. But this was then the established Philadelphia method, although I believe it does not prevail so extensively now.

The results in this case appear to have been good. Whether they might have been better or not under a different system, it is useless to conjecture. But the very title of the texts and subjects then presented gives us an indication of the sort of work that was done. " Christ seeking the lost sheep "; " When he saw him afar off"; " One thing thou lackest "; " The Spirit and the bride say come ";   **Revival Texts.**
" He made haste and came down "; " Remember me when thou comest into thy kingdom "; " Almost thou persuadest me to be a Christian "; " Salvation is from the Lord "; " Lovest thou me ? " " How long halt ye ? " These were some of the texts and themes preached in those services. And at their close, at the regular communion of March, 1870, a company of thirty persons stood up and confessed their Saviour.

VIII.

Dr. Breed's personal habits were very systematic, and his home life a pleasant and charming one. In Steubenville his Mondays were given almost exclusively to frolic and fun with his children, or to needful rest. On Tuesday he locked the door of his study. The little footsteps and the baby voices were excluded from the hallway, and he gave himself during the rest of the mornings of the week to study. After an early dinner he devoted himself to pastoral work; and at night, when public engagements did not require him, he was found with his family striving, by various arts of which he was master, to make them happy. His first strength and service were for his Church, and then for his family; and few children have better cause to remember their father with love and gratitude. In Philadelphia, this was substantially his habit. His sexton always knew that he could clean the study on Monday, as the Doctor was never there, and although as years went on changes inevitably came into the family life, he kept on the even tenor of his way, working in the morning, visiting in the afternoon, and resting in his household at night.

Personal Characteristics.

Dr. Breed was a thorough Presbyterian by conviction, both on principle and as the result of experience. He believed that in the organization of our Church there were all the possibilities of successful work for Christ. His general practice as to church government may be summed up in a few sentences. He protested on the one hand against what he called the "semi-prelacy" of pastoral domination or autocracy; and, on the other hand, against that Independency shown by frequent appeals to the people for settlement of questions which the Session ought to decide. The pastor and elders are appointed to rule, and they ought to rule in spiritual things with firmness and tenderness, with a full knowledge and conviction of their rightful powers, and at the same time with a full

Views on Church Government.

understanding of and deference towards the powers of the congregation. A Presbyterian Church is a representative republic, in which the authority that under God vests in the people is relegated to certain officers elected by them and ordained for that purpose. Under this conception all the spiritual interests of Dr. Breed's Church were controlled by the pastor and ruling elders. For example, the superintendent of the Sunday School was an officer of the church, appointed by the Session, and when he withdrew from office his resignation was to the Session, and while in office, he was held responsible to the Session for whatever was done and taught in the school. By this mode of government, the excitement, partisanship and divisions which have sometimes attended frequent elections in the Sabbath School were avoided.

In the matter of worship he was a strict Puritan. His sympathies were not with the more liberal Presbyterianism of the Continent, or even the earlier Presbyterianism of the English-speaking churches, but rather with some of its later developments, as under the Cov- **Worship.** enanters, and the stern and barren cultus of Puritanism. The Geneva gown, which is the pulpit robe of our forefathers, and is universally worn to-day in the parent churches of Great Britain and the Continent, he long looked upon with disrelish ; but in the last few years of life he desired to see it restored to our preachers. His idea of a church cultus included little of the formal or ritual, although, strange to say, he was the author of a handbook for funerals, to take the very place which a Book of Forms supplies.

He was fond of music. He himself had written a number of hymns, especially for the use of the children. Flowers he loved dearly, and took the greatest pleasure in searching them out and pressing them for preservation. Yet he could speak in the following terms **Church Music.** of the use of music in the praise of God, and of flowers for the decoration of the sanctuary : "We have steadily avoided the tendency that in some cases has resulted in a sort of combination of the religious opera and the horticultural exhibition. And we trust that the day is yet a good way off when our people will be found decking their worship with any of the ribbons of a fantastic ritualism, or straying into the flower-fringed path that so often terminates at Rome." As to special and professional singing in the sanctuary, he had little patience with it, and in speaking of it characterized it as "yielding up the singing gallery to the musical artiste, according to whose creed the chief end of the Church is the organ loft, and the chief end of the performers there is to display their accomplishments, sing their own praises and gratify their cultivated musical taste, and the effect of which is to fritter away the attention, thought, emotion due to the stupendous themes of righteousness, temperance and judgment to come." *

Yet he never had a bitter word against those of us who represent (or claim to represent) the more catholic American Pan-Presbyterianism, and were not in sympathy with his views; but he uttered his opinions with a pleasant smile and clothed their point with a bright pun, a witty saying, or a humorous anecdote, that took away whatever of sting might have been in them.

On the matter of deacons, he had strong opinions, and considered no Church perfectly organized until it had introduced these Scriptural and Presbyterian offices. He emphasized the fact that the first officers ordained after the apostles, were not elders, but deacons, whose one great duty it was to take care of the poor. He pointed to the fact that this spirit pervaded the early Church; and while as the centuries rolled on, every other office of the Church was modified and distorted almost beyond recognition, the office of deacons remained long unchanged in its original form, signification and function. He magnified that law of the Presbyterian Church that no one of its members should be allowed to suffer for the

Views on Deacons.

---

* Historical Discourse, p. 24.

necessaries of life, and that they should not be thrown upon the charity of others. It was not simply for the sake of organic symmetry and conformity to the requirements of Christ and the Church that he advocated the diaconate, but that the command of Christ might be fully observed and the poor of the Christian brotherhood be clothed with the mantle of Christian love.*

This deep-rooted devotion to the order and worship of the Presbyterian Church was associated with a profound pride in its noble history. He had read widely and well the records of the various branches of our one ecclesiastical family, and his mind was in touch with all that was great and worthy in their **Pride in Presbyterian History.** achievements. The bitter persecutions of the primitive Waldensians among the beautiful mountain valleys of Piedmont ; the conflicts and sufferings of the Huguenots of France, in the days when the noblest of the realm were marshalled under Admiral Coligny in the love and defence of Truth ; the world-reaching influence of Calvin, Geneva and the Protestant cantons of Switzerland; the noble record of the Reformed people of the Palatinate, along the banks of the sunny Rhine ; the exciting struggles of the handful of Holland's brave heroes, under William the Silent, to hold their sea-swept land against the assaults of King Philip II and Bloody Alva ; the story of Knox and his compeers ; of the hunted Covenanters on the heathered hills of Scotland in the days when Archbishop Laud's bitter hand was pressed hard against them; the uprising of the clans as an echo of the thud of Jennie Geddes's stool in the old Cathedral of St. Giles ; the splendid story, with its sad termination, of the days when Presbyterianism held the reins of government in England and brought in perfidious Charles II, to find that it had put a serpent into its bosom to sting it to death,—these and other historic

---

* See Historical Discourse, pp. 22, 23.

records of the mighty conflicts for political and religious liberty, in which Presbyterians led the van and bore the brunt, were familiar to him; and many of us have felt his power to stir the heart with the too little known tale of the noble ancestors of our American Presbyterian Church.

This feeling found apt expression in two great movements. The first was the erection of the Witherspoon statue. A casual suggestion in the columns of a religious newspaper, the "Presbyterian," of this city, caught Dr. Breed's eye and wrought within him the purpose of erecting a statue to Dr. John Witherspoon, in commemoration of the 100th anniversary of the Republic. This he regarded as a fitting way to recall the attention of our own people, and as far as possible the people of the land, to the part that Presbyterians had taken in creating and giving character to the Republic. So prominent was that part that Mr. Galloway, in the British House of Commons, denounced the whole Revolution as "a Presbyterian movement." The Sons of Liberty in the City of New York, went by the name of the "Presbyterian Junto." Mr. Bancroft writes: "The first voice publicly raised in America to dissolve all connection with Great Britain came not from the Puritans of New England, nor from the Dutch of New York, nor from the planters of Virginia, but from the Scotch-Irish Presbyterians.* That voice was heard in what is known as "The Mecklenburg Declaration" among the Presbyterians of North Carolina. During the time that the Carolinas were occupied by the British troops, every Presbyterian Church was systematically burned, on the theory that it was a nest of treason. In the Congress that created this Republic there was but one clergyman, and he in his person ably represented the combined Presbyterianism of the land. "It will not be questioned," said Dr. Breed, "that in this hour when the fate of the colonies was trembling in the balance, his eloquent voice told mightily for the cause of independence; nor will it be questioned that

Witherspoon Statue.

in the even more solemn and difficult matter of organization, his influence was of incaluable value.*"

Animated by such views, Dr. Breed began the work of raising the money required to rear the Witherspoon Monument. Dr. Boardman gave his earnest and cordial sympathy and influence. Others cheered on the task, but the whole of the work fell upon Dr. Breed. By exchanging pulpits on Wednesday evenings and Sabbaths, and by working during his summer vacations, he presented the subject in more than seventy pulpits, in ten Synods and Presbyteries, stretching from the Atlantic coast to Ohio. With the exception of the First Presbyterian Church in New York, of which Professor Paxton, of Princeton, was then pastor, his own church, besides doing all the work through its pastor, contributed also by far the largest amount of money for this enterprise. No one will ever know how vast was the toil and how great the care out of which this work was consummated. When the contemplated changes in the position of that statue shall have been finished, it will be fitting to inscribe upon some part of the pedestal that bears aloft the noble effigy these words: "This monument was erected chiefly through the zeal and labors of William Pratt Breed."

The same spirit found course through the Presbyterian Historical Society, located in this city, and of whose Executive Committee he was the Chairman. In fact, *he* was, in large part, the Historical Society. The last letter which I received from him was a reminder of a promise made to give him, for the museum in the Library Hall of that institution, one of the so-called "communion stanes of Irongray," which I had brought with me from that mountain valley in Dumfriesshire, Scotland, where the harried and hunted Covenanters held their farewell communion in the "killing days," as they have been called, of 1678.

Historical Society.

---

* See Historical Discourse, p. 39.

The last public service of his life was in the lecture room of his own beloved Church, and the motive of that discourse was his historical interest in the life and labors of the missionary, Brainard. He had received certain memorials of this sainted Apostle to the Indians, to be placed among the historic treasures of his well beloved Society, and these were presented as objective illustrations of this last service.

An interest attaches to that last service which as yet is known to but a

His Last Service.

few. Dr. Breed had formed the deliberate purpose to do for the Church and its Historical Society a work similar to that which he had accomplished for the Witherspoon monument. He hoped that God would permit him, as the last work of his life, and the crowning of all his days, to be the instrument in procuring a sum of money that would erect and endow a suitable library and museum hall in which the books and treasures of the society could be safely and reputably housed. He had prepared that lecture with these things in his mind. His plan of campaign was all laid out, and he was just ready to enter upon it when the hand of death struck him. We can better gather his purpose from his own words. A few days before his death, while lying quite ignorant of the serious danger of his disease, his eldest son entered his room, and with cheerful words congratulated his father upon seeming to be so much better. " Yes, yes," was the answer. " Dr. Woods must get me out of this! I want to go through the pulpits of the country, if the brethren will open them to me, for I have got the endorsement of Dr. John Hall, and I think I can raise the $250,000 endowment fund for the Presbyterian Historical Society." Alas, this hope, which spanned like a rainbow his closing days, was not to be realized for him. Yet may we not indulge the trust that this last purpose for the Church's welfare shall not pass stillborn from the earth? Shall not we, his associates and friends, take up and push it forward to its consummation? May the echoes of that voice, now silenced in the grave, linger still within the conch shell of Brainard and roll in echoes through the land, summoning all loyal Presbyterian hearts to the noble undertaking which was breathed into its convolutions by the dying breath of Breed!

If I were asked to suggest what would be the most fitting monument to our beloved brother, I should answer—a new Library Hall and Museum room for the Presbyterian Historical **His Best Monument.** Society. Such a memorial might well be located in some more fitting site than the present edifice, where it could be associated with a lecture hall, reading and social rooms, and other conveniences for Presbyterial assemblages and the monthly gatherings of that Church club which has recently been organized in our city.

IX.

A striking characteristic of Dr. Breed was his mirthfulness. Persons who did not know him well, would hardly have suspected that this quality was so strongly developed in him. But the familiars of **Mirthfulness.** his home circle, and those ministerial friends who were privileged to come near him in social life, understood it well. I have more than once been strongly amused at the surprise which would come over a group of ministers in a general audience, as some flash of wit, or curious turn of speech, or mirthful phrase, or playful pun would drop from the lips of the solemn and dignified gentleman who was addressing them. One such scene I recall at the General Assembly which met, in 1870, at the First Church, on Washington Square, and which was known as the "Reunion Assembly." In the closing hours of that body it fell to Dr. Breed to make some farewell remarks; and the manner in which he took up a number of prominent members of that venerable body, and played upon their names with well turned puns, was keenly enjoyed. But one of the most amusing features of the scene was the startled sur-

5

prise of groups and individuals here and there, as they straightened up and leaned forward, and then, catching the mirthful spirit of the man, gave way by very reaction to hearty enjoyment of his address.

Very recently, indeed, since he retired from the active pastorate, he gave our brethren of New York a similar surprise. His address at an important Church gathering was represented to me by a leading layman of our sister city as full of wit, sparkling with humor, and one of the happiest addresses he had ever listened to. It was to my informant, as to the majority of those who heard, a revelation of a most unexpected faculty. Probably the very last thing that he wrote, and which was penned or typed within a week of his death, was one of the wittiest that he ever conceived, and will never be forgotten by the circle of friends for whose benefit it was composed. There can be no doubt that had he chosen to give literary exercise to this faculty, he would have achieved a place among the very foremost humorous writers of the country. Yet, as long as I have known Dr. Breed, and we were ordained by the same Presbytery of Steubenville, and I have known him from my boyhood, I never heard, and never knew any man who heard the slightest departure from the strictest line of purity and dignity in the exercise of a faculty which sometimes leads its possessors astray. This was a good gift of God to him, and lightened many of his burdens, and cheered many of the hours of his discouragements. There is nothing inconsistent in the possession and highest exercise of such a faculty, with that tender sympathy which marked his character and made him so eminently a friend of the sorrowing. Indeed, the two faculties lie close by each other in the human mind. The poet has well sung :—

> " So closely our whims on our miseries tread,
> That the laugh is awaked ere the tear can be dried."

Dr. Breed held the pen of a ready writer. His literary life was chiefly in the line of that department of our Church's work which is represented by the Board of Publication, of which for so many years he was the honored President. Nearly forty titles of **Literary Work.** publications of varying importance may be found upon the catalogue of that corporation under the name of Dr. Breed. Most of these are bound volumes, and they have had a wide circulation among the special classes for whom they were prepared. They have added greatly to the usefulness of his life, and will aid to perpetuate that usefulness now that his busy pen is forever still. For years he has been the Philadelphia correspondent of the New York *Evangelist*, and his letters have been a most interesting feature of that journal to which its Philadelphia readers, especially, were almost always sure to turn first.

Dr. Breed had a strong love for nature in all her various forms. Earlier in his life he had taken up a specialty in entomology, and pursued it with some degree of success. He was long a member of the American Entomological Society, whose home is in this city, and **As a Naturalist.** was also enrolled in the membership of our Academy of Natural Sciences. Though he ceased years ago active membership in these two organizations, he never lost his fondness for Natural History, and for the living things of God in the great world of natural life. Those who came in close contact with him, and those who listened to him most carefully, must have observed how frequently he drew his illustrations and suggestive thoughts from this realm of the Great Creator.

He was especially interested in the order of insects known as the Lepidoptera, including moths and butterflies, and made a large, and in some features, a valuable collection of those animals. A friend who traveled with him in Europe during a six months' tour,—one of the very bright spots of Dr. Breed's life, has described the outbreaks of his collector's enthusiasm even amid the attractions of the old world. Dr. Breed, who was a ready rhymster, as well as a keen wit and inveterate punster, wrote in verse and read one evening in a hotel parlor, some humorous incidents of the trip, indulging in a little fun at the expense of his fellow travelers. One of his companions, a child of this church, and now a member of the congregation,* responded a little later with a somewhat similar paper, a part of which I quote as giving us a picture of our friend on one of his collecting tours.

> " The pilgrim carried a staff and a cane,
> One for the mountain and one for the plain ;
> Of maps and guide books he had great store,
> Pockets he stuffed till they'd hold no more ;
> From every ruin a flower he took,
> And pressed it with care in a little book.

> " At Interlaken he might have been seen
> Chasing gay butterflies over the green,
> With a rod and a net to catch his prey,
> And a paper box to stow them away,
> But before boxing up the insects dumb,
> He put them to death with finger and thumb,
> And said, with a smile, to each pretty fly—
> ' Don't think me cruel because you must die !
> Not for sport, but for science, I'm acting thus !
> So die like a martyr, and don't make a fuss ;
> On a shelf I will put you, when I reach home,
> With saintly relics I've brought from Rome.' "

When he greatly widened the sphere of his parish work, and those catholic labors for the Church which fall upon many city pastors compelled him to give up his specialty, he turned over his collection to a young nephew who had been inoculated with the naturalist's fever of research by his enthusiastic relative. That nephew as his years ripened developed into a thoroughly equipped Lepidopterist, made his uncle's gift the basis of a noble collection, won for himself, and still holds, a not. inconspicuous place among American entomologists.

* Rev. Dr. Francis J. Collier.

During the bright summer which he spent with his wife at Ventnor, whither he had been sent by his loving people just after the sickness which led to his final retirement, he gave free course to his love for nature. The greater part of his vacation was spent in wandering through the fields, drinking in fresh air from shore and sea, and communing with nature in all her varied forms. Byron's well known lines express his feelings :—

Ventnor Vacation.

> "I love not man the less, but nature more
> For these her solitudes, in which I steal
> From all I may be or have been before,
> To mingle with the universe and feel
> What I cannot express, yet may not all conceal."

During these wanderings, he gathered quantities of grasses and flowers, which he carefully pressed in the well known methods of the botanist, and mounted and packed away. These were brought to America and cherished by many to whom they were sent as mementoes of his Ventnor visit.

Dr. Breed was a man of great tenderness of heart. His sympathy was keen and deep. Those of his people who have passed through trial know what a friend he was to them in their hour of need, and how his love, like that of a father or a brother, encompassed them with the tenderest and holiest offices of his ministry.

Sympathy.

It was this quality that made him pre-eminently a pastor of his flock. Grave, serious, somewhat stiff in his outward manner, let but some sorrow fall, his whole nature responded, lit up as the rugged outlines of some mountain under the glow and warmth of a rising sun, and he was alive in all his being to those touches of Nature which make the whole world kin.

One of his elders, Mr John D. McCord, informed me that during a long confinement as the result of a serious accident, Dr. Breed never

failed a day, *for three months*, to call at his house and offer prayer at his
bedside. One might challenge the entire history of the Church for an
example of pastoral devotion and friendship superior to that!

X.

"On the top of the pillars was lily-work." Thus the sacred writer
describes the two columns, Jakin and Boaz, that were set at the "Beau-

The Summary. tiful Gate" of the temple of Israel. They represented
attributes of the supreme God of the Hebrews, and
exhibited that character which He sought to develop by the services of
his house within his people. The pillar was the emblem of strength,
the lily-work of the beauty which adorned it, and thus strength and
beauty were in the sanctuary.

I know no text that can better describe my own conception of the
sanctuary of that life which so lately stood among us in its manly beauty,
and which has been taken hence by the Master-Architect to add to the
garnishing and perfecting of that building of God, the spiritual temple,
eternal in the heavens: Pillars and lily-work—strength and beauty!

Dr. Breed was a manly man. His physical appearance would scarcely
have given one the impression of robustness, yet he was really physically
strong, rarely sick throughout his long life, and always ready for duty.

"Pillars." His slight frame was endowed with a large share of
natural vigor and vitality. But his strength was especially
in character, conviction and purpose to do good. The peculiar erectness
of his body, which struck every observer, was a fair type of the upright-
ness of his character and the orthodoxy of his faith. There was no
more broadly catholic clergyman within our Church, which, to say the
least, is not inconspicuous in the sisterhood of Christendom for the
catholicity of its communion. He loved the whole Church of God, under

whatever name called. He was tolerant toward all forms of faith that seemed to him loyal to the fundamental principles of religion. But there was no man who more sincerely loved, more earnestly cherished and more vigorously defended the doctrine and polity of the Church in whose holy ministry he served. Gentle as were all his ways, considerate and tender towards his fellow men, we have seen him stand like a rock in the defence of truths which he regarded vital to the cause of Christ.

All his characteristics were dominated by conscience and piety. He was a man of tender conscience, quick to turn at every suggestion of duty and to spurn every appearance of evil. He was a man of God. He walked with God. His piety was unobtrusive, but it was of that subtle quality, which made itself acknowledged by all with whom he came in contact. There was nothing of cant or hypocrisy about him. He never flaunted his convictions in the face of friends, nor made broad his phylacteries before the Church, nor flung the banner of his faith upon the outer wall of the world, to flutter and beat in the faces of passers by. But he so lived, that men felt in his presence that they were near to one who was near to Christ. Xenophon in his Cryopædia, never once says in direct terms that Cyrus

Lily-work.

was great, but he so wrote that every chapter deepened upon the mind of the reader the truth that among the leaders of his day, there was none greater than Cyrus. So was it in the life of our beloved friend and father. He never obtruded in direct terms his allegiance to Christ, but the outflowering and fragrance of his life left wherever he went the unmistakable impression that to him Christ his Lord was the Chiefest among ten thousand, and the one altogether lovely. God was to him the over-mastering element of life, and all the springs of his being were in Him whom he adored and served. He sought to see God, and he saw God immanent in Nature, in Providence, in History, in Church, in the Kingdom and word of Grace, in the Family, in Social Life; and now he has passed on and upward to the Beatific Vision, and henceforth forever shall see God face to face.

From the scenes of earthly labor to the sphere of eternal rest, God hath removed him who lately walked and wrought among us. Our sorrow is tempered with gratitude when we remember

Lessons From His Life. the life he was privileged to live, and the example which he has left. In the fullness of Christian character, few of his generation of ministers have excelled him. How few have equaled him we who were his nearest friends and associates freely allow.

You have visited the studio of an artist-friend and found pleasurable engagement in watching the development of various pictures. There is a canvas on which the background has been laid in, and only here and and there a hump or splash of color, a flowing line, a shade, a gleam of light, mark the outlines of a picture that is to be. Here is a second study on which the motif just begins to show from the crude figures. A third picture is yet further developed, and the master hand appears in the growing forms, proportions, colors. Ah! here is another study! We may stop and admire it. Even the artist will welcome our gaze and criticism. His work is nearly finished. A little more shadow at this point; a little more light at that; a touch of color on yonder hill top; more sunshine in yonder sky, and the master may write his name on the canvas, and the gilder may frame it and bear it away to hang in the gallery with kindred works of art; aye, if you please, in the very palace of the King!

In the gallery of God's Church, where the Divine Artist is painting upon the background of human character the holy images of a heavenly life, there are diversities of developments. Here the crude beginnings of a Christian life; there the more advanced attainment of one who has been years under the forming hand of the Holy Ghost; but here one, whose life is nearly done, before whom the Church, aye, and the world, may stand and say, "Mark the perfect man, and behold the upright"! Such was Dr. Breed. He was among us as one on whom the hand of the Spirit Divine had wrought earth's fairest work. From the background of his life there stood out the spiritual picture of a soul redeemed and fashioned into the image of the Son of God. There needed yet the finishing touches, the shadows of earth to be obliterated, the sunshine of sanctifying grace in preparation for Heaven, and then, framed in stainless immortality, he has found place in the palace of our Heavenly King! Let us strive, as we follow his upward flight, and cry, like Elisha of old, "My Father, my Father, the chariot of Israel and the horsemen thereof," so to use the opportunities of life, and accept the grace of Heaven that we, like him, may grow in grace and in the knowledge of our Lord and Saviour, Christ.

Many of you last saw him as he raised the conch shell of holy Brainard the missionary, to his lips, and made an ineffectual effort to reawaken therein the sounds that had summoned the red men to the following of Jesus. May I not, with this closing vision in mind, give for you the lesson which an American poet has heard in the murmurs of another shell of the ocean—the chambered nautilus:—

> " Build thee more stately mansions, O my soul !
> As the swift seasons roll,
> Leave thy low vaulted Past !
> Let each new temple, nobler than the last,
> Shut thee from Heaven with a dome more vast,
> Till thou at length art free,
> Leaving thine outgrown shell by Life's unresting sea ! "

I close this memorial discourse of a life so beautiful, so saintly, so serviceable to man, with the words with which our friend ended his Quarter-century Discourse :—

" And the future, how well we know it ! A brief period of alternating work and rest, peace and anxiety, sorrow and joy, health and sickness, pleasure and pain :

> ' And when the work is done,
> When the last soul is won,
> When Jesus' love and power
> Have cheered the dying hour ;
> Oh ! then the crown is given,
> Oh ! then the rest in heaven !
> Endless life is endless day,
> Sin and sorrow passed away.' "

MINUTES AND RESOLUTIONS.

Minute adopted by the Session of the West Spruce Street Presbyterian Church :—

At a called meeting of the Session of the West Spruce Street Presbyterian Church of Philadelphia, held February 15th, 1889, the following Minute was adopted :—

The Reverend William Pratt Breed, D.D., the first and only pastor of this church, died in the early morning of Thursday, the fourteenth day of February, A. D. 1889, at his residence, No. 258 South Sixteenth street, in the city of Philadelphia, after a brief illness of one week, in the 73d year of his age. The Session desire to place upon permanent record its high appreciation of the services, character and work of its beloved pastor and presiding officer. He was unanimously called to the pastorate of this church on the third day of April, A. D. 1856, and was duly installed on the fourth day of June, A. D. 1856. For more than thirty-one years and five months he performed the duties of his high office with a zeal, a devotion, a degree of spirituality, and an entire consecration to the cause of his Master and the best interests of this church, which have had few equals and no superiors in any similar work. With some of the present members of the Session he has been associated during almost the whole of his pastorate, and with all of them for many years. They all testify that, during the whole period of their association it has been a joy to them ; and no jar or dissonance, or divided vote or action, has ever at any time been experienced. The gentleness, the transparency of his character, the sweetness of his temper, his unselfishness, his singleness of purpose, the consecration of his whole being and powers to his Master's work among us, have been such that we cannot speak of them in terms of too high praise. He has labored with a devotion and earnestness which have borne great fruit and endeared him to all the people of his charge. And when advancing years and their infirmities induced him, in November, 1887, to tender to the congregation his resignation, it was accepted, only upon the condition that he should continue to be their pastor *emeritus*, and that his support during the remainder of his life should be their continual pleasure and care. His last service was in our lecture room on the evening of February 6th, and with much of his old earnestness and fervor he told of the great missionary, David Brainard, whom in so very many respects he so much resembled. With those of us whose privilege it was to be then present, those last words of his will be a pleasant memory. We will ever cherish the recollection of our pastor's life, character and labors as one of our most hallowed treasures.

Attest : FRANK K. HIPPLE, *Clerk of Session.*

77

Minute adopted by the Board of Trustees of the West Spruce Street Presbyterian Church :—

The Board of Trustees of the West Spruce Street Presbyterian Church, participating in this deepest and greatest sorrow of our church, would record this Minute upon the death of a beloved pastor, the Reverend William Pratt Breed, D.D. Thirty years and more have passed since he was divinely led to our church as its *first pastor;* and in all these years, covering a pastorate almost exceptional as to duration, he has gone in and out before us as the man of God, pure and undefiled, clothed as with the mantle of Christ's righteousness and humility, a High Priest of the Lord, ever ministering as from the altar in the inner sanctuary where the Shekinah dwelleth. He was the courteous gentleman, honoring social life by his presence ; his footstep was the welcome sound upon the threshold of every home ; his genial manner made each fireside to glow with greater brightness ; and his companionship was a pleasure always to be desired, filled as it was with the riches of a cultivated mind and a refined humor. His patriotism was of that type that made his love of country second only to his love of God. Intensely an American, he stood in the pulpit and on the rostrum as a champion of liberty and freedom, the defender of his country's Constitution and his country's flag, the exemplar of a loyal citizen. His friendship,—how is it to be valued ? Kindly by nature, embellished with Christian love, no unkind word had he for his fellows,—generous to others' faults, he was beloved by all, and leaves no enemy to mar this Christ-like legacy. As the *only pastor* of this church—his ministrations were divinely blest, and many stars will adorn his crown. Though called from us and from earth, his life-work will follow him into the generations to come, through the agency of those he led from death to life. His example pervaded the Church and its work, and hence, through all these years, its harmony has been undisturbed. He was inseparably woven into every family circle, entwined around every heart, and we can but bow in submission, as he has taught us, to the will of his God and our God ; and yet with grateful hearts, for his long pastorate, his useful and honored life, and mingling our tears with the Church, the ministry, our fellow-citizens, our fellow-parishioners, and the sorely bereaved family, triumphantly exclaim, amid our united sorrow, " He was faithful unto death."

Extract from the Minutes.   CHARLES O. ABBEY, *Secretary.*

From the Minutes of the Presbytery of Philadelphia, April 1st, 1889 :—

Thursday morning, February 14th, 1889, Rev. William Pratt Breed, D.D., passed to his rest, after an illness of just one week.

Dr. Breed was received into the Presbytery of Philadelphia from the Presbytery of Steubenville, Ohio, May 26th, 1856. On June 4th of the same year he was installed Pastor of the West Spruce Street Church and continued in this relation until November 7th, 1887, when, at his own urgent request, on account of failing strength, he was released. His congregation acquiesced only upon the condition that he should become Pastor-emeritus, and that his support during the remainder of his life should be their continuing pleasure and care. To the last he lived among his people and worshipped with them, preaching and lecturing on Wednesday evenings, and performing such pastoral duties as his strength permitted.

As a preacher, Dr. Breed was always interesting, always instructive, always tender. As a pastor he was almost paternal in his thought and care for his people. The record of his house-to-house ministry, if it could be written, would be full of beautiful experiences and tender incidents.

As a Presbyter he was faithful and diligent. He took a deep interest in the affairs of the Presbytery, especially in whatever concerned the extension of the Master's kingdom. In his relations with his brethren he was cordial, kindly and thoughtful, interested in their work and ready ever to lend a hand, quick in sympathy with those who were discouraged or in trouble, and faithful in his friendships.

His life was singularly beautiful, well-rounded and complete. He ripened into the full fruitage of years, of labor, of usefulness. He saw his work finished. He suffered no painful wrench in his circumstances, such as ofttimes in old age tears a godly minister away from his people and from the work of his life, but was permitted to remain in the midst of the associations of long, happy years, and among those for whom he had labored and prayed,—honored, beloved, revered. Never had pastor more loyal and affectionate parishioners, and to the last it was their joy to give him comfort and care. He passed no long period of physical and mental decay, such as in many cases marks the ending of good men's lives, but was permitted to continue in the active service of his Lord almost to the very close.

We will cherish his name and memory, for there is nothing in his life that we would want to forget. We shall miss his presence and his counsel, but his work remains, not alone in the noble church which has known no other pastor, but in the abiding influence which he has exerted upon the church universal. We should all be better, purer in heart, gentler in speech, holier in life, more earnest in every good work, for having lived so long under the hallowed influence of his Christ-like life.

The Presbytery of Philadelphia unanimously adopted the foregoing Minute by a rising vote, and directed the Stated Clerk to transmit a copy thereof to the Session of the West Spruce Street Church.

By order of the Presbytery.   W. M. RICE, *Stated Clerk.*

Minute adopted by the Presbyterian Ministerial Association, Philadelphia, at a meeting held Monday, March 11th, in the Assembly Room, 1334 Chestnut street. Prepared by a committee of three, one from each Presbytery :—

The Rev. William P. Breed, D.D., a member of this Association, entered upon his rest and reward on the morning of Thursday, February 14th, 1889, in the 73d year of his age.

It is with sad yet trusting hearts that we record the departure from this life of our brother. He was a diligent student, an instructive preacher, and a devoted and earnest pastor; but the members of this Association will especially remember him as their beloved friend. Although not absolutely engaged in the active work of the pastorate during the last few months of his life, yet our brother was at this time at the very height of his usefulness, affecting by his speech, his pen, and his life, a wider circle than ever before. God buries the workmen, but carries on the work. The works of this servant of God "do follow him," and hence it is cause both for thankfulness and hope that his life and example shall still speak after many, many days.

Dr. Breed was accustomed to make careful preparation for the pulpit. He was, as some of us know, regularly, when not kept from the place by some urgent pastoral engagement, to be found at his table in his study at the church upon the morning of every working day of the week. The only exception he made was upon those Monday mornings when, with his brethren, he sought recreation and encouragement, and real help for his work, in this Association of Ministers. He was heard to say a short time before his death, when asked where he would have his study when another pastor would be chosen for the West Spruce Street Church: "Ah, my dear people will never deprive me of that place, which they know I love so well."

His ministrations were characterized by great reverence for the Word of God, and ready submission to its authority; and therefore, while closely adhering to the "form of sound words," his sermons were much relished by hearers, in his own and other congregations, who "desired the sincere milk of the Word."

In the social circle his presence was ever welcome. His lovely, beaming face, his cheerful disposition, his rare intellectual endowments, his sparkling wit, made him attractive not only to his ministerial brethren, but also in all society.

Dr. Breed was truly a model pastor, "instant in season and out of season." He regarded pastoral visitation, and especially attending upon his people when in sickness and sorrow, as a most important part of his work as a minister of the Gospel. Hence his labors in this direction were unremitting, and the full and blessed results of this beloved pastor's visits in Philadelphia and Steubenville, Ohio, the great day alone will reveal.

In prayer, whether in the sanctuary, the social meeting, or the home, our friend exhibited extraordinary power and unction; and coming, as he no doubt did, each Sabbath morning fresh from the Sacred Presence, it is no wonder that his manner in the pulpit was always so solemn and impressive.

Dr. Breed was a man of ripe scholarship and eminent culture; of high theological and literary attainments; he was an excellent historian; a man well read in the various departments of science, but unlike many with less acquirements, his native modesty constantly prevented him from making an unusual display of his various acquisitions.

Our brother was endowed with a calm yet acute judgment; his counsel we felt could be relied upon. Ah! how we shall feel the loss of that counsel in this Ministerial Association, in the Presbytery, and in the various institutions of the Church with which he was connected.

The fatal illness which seized him upon his return to his home after that Wednesday evening service of prayer and rejoicing with his dear people, only lasted for a week, and then the saintly spirit of one of the most dearly beloved and faithful ministers of Christ we have ever known joined the heavenly choir and the innumerable company. It seems to us who still linger here that we cannot make him dead. It is hard to realize that we shall never again see him in yonder seat, that we shall no more in this upper room hear the earnest tones of that voice which was always uttered in defence of that which is honorable and true. But while this bereavement brings with it much of sadness and even darkness, let us, as ministers of Christ, not "sorrow even as others that have no hope." Let us rejoice that our brother was distinguished for the purity of his principles and the transparency of his character. That he walked with God in life and sank to his bed unshadowed by a cloud ; and hence we may say that he is now "present with the Lord."

Let us rejoice that we have the sure and certain hope of meeting our friend again, when the mysteries of Providence shall be explained by the revelation of its marvelous issues ; when the morning shall break and the shadows flee away, all but that one bright, blessed *shadow*, "for he who dwelleth in the secret place of the Most High shall abide (forever abide) under the shadow of the Almighty."

This Association devoutly prays that God's blessing, which our departed brother so constantly and earnestly invoked upon all his friends whom he cherished so fondly in life, may rest upon his bereaved family, the church of which he was so long the honored pastor, and upon all his brethren in the ministry.

> Rev. J. Addison Henry, D.D.,
> Rev. Joseph Beggs, D.D., } *Committee.*
> Rev. Wm. Hutton,

Minute adopted by the Synod of Pennsylvania, in Session at Altoona, Pa., October, 1889. Your Committee appointed to prepare a suitable Minute of respect for the memory of Rev. William P. Breed, D.D., would respectfully report as follows :—

The Synod of Pennsylvania, in session at Altoona, records its tribute of respect for the memory of Rev. William Pratt Breed, D. D., Moderator of this Synod at its meeting in Pittsburgh, in 1883, and, before the consolidation of the Synods twice Moderator of the old Synod of Philadelphia, and who, full of years and honors, on the 14th of February, 1889, had his membership transferred from the Church and its courts here on earth to the General Assembly and Church of the First-born whose names are written in heaven.

Dr. Breed was born at Greenbush, N. Y., August 23d, 1816; united with the Church in 1832; graduated from the University of New York in 1843, and from

Princeton Theological Seminary in 1847; pastor of the Second Presbyterian Church, Steubenville, Ohio, from 1847 to 1856, and pastor of the West Spruce Street Presbyterian Church from 1856 till his death, in Philadelphia, last February, the last year being as pastor emeritus.

As a preacher Dr. Breed was interesting and effective, and as a pastor he was faithful and successful. Nearly 400 united with his church during his first pastorate, and in Philadelphia over 1100. As an author he was brilliant and instructive. Not less than seventeen volumes came from his pen, besides a large number of tracts and numerous newspaper articles. As a laborer in "outside work," he was one of the most prominent promoters and efficient co-workers. The Witherspoon monument, in Fairmount Park, Philadelphia, which sprang from his earnest efforts, and which was practically his work, is a specimen of his abundant labors. As a Presbyter he wielded a strong influence, whether in his Presbytery, or in this Synod, or in the General Assembly, of which he was frequently a member, or in the Councils of the Pan-Presbyterian Alliance, in all of which he was a member, except the last. As a presiding officer he was faithful and efficient. He was President of the Board of Publication and Sabbath-school Work of our Church for many years, and his earnest voice was often heard in its behalf, and many successful appeals came from his able and brilliant pen for its prosperity. As a Christian gentleman, he was kind, gentle, courteous, considerate, a man whom none knew but to love and revere, whose presence was always a benediction. Dr. Breed will ever be remembered by those who knew him as a true friend and a wise counselor, as a beautiful type of a Christian man and a noble specimen of a consecrated minister.

Dr. Breed's remarkable success in the various positions which he held is due to his versatility of talent, his variety of attainment, his tact in administration, his prudence in all matters, his facility in writing, his felicity in expression, his cheerfulness in manner, his purity of heart, his beauty of holiness, his devotion to the Master's work, his adherence to God's truth, and his faith in the Lord Jesus Christ.

The Synod of Pennsylvania rejoices in the success and value of his manifold and fruitful labors, which will perpetuate his memory in the Church, in its judicatories, and the various other religious organizations with which he was identified; and the Synod also rejoices in the fact that it bestowed upon him the highest proof of its regard and affection by calling him to the Moderator's chair six years ago. While absent from the Church and its judicatories here below, we rejoice to think of him as present with the Lord in the General Assembly of the Church above.

While sincerely sorrowing for the great loss it has sustained, the Synod sincerely extends to the family of Dr. Breed its heartfelt sympathies.

Resolved, That a copy of this minute, attested by the Stated Clerk, be sent to the family of Dr. Breed.

Respectfully submitted,

Attest: IRWIN P. McCURDY, *Chairman.*

JAMES ROBERTS, *Stated Clerk of Synod.*

Extract from the Minutes of The Presbyterian Board of Publication and Sabbath-school Work, in Special Session, February 16th, 1889 :—

Upon motion it was *Resolved*, That a Committee of three be appointed to prepare a Minute expressive of the views of the Board in reference to the death of its President, the Rev. W. P. Breed, D. D., to report at the next meeting of the Board.

Resolved, That as a testimonial of respect for his memory the store be closed during the funeral services, on Monday, from ten to one o'clock, and that the members, officers, and employees of the Board attend the funeral services.

Resolved, That in further respect to his memory the office of President be kept vacant until the coming annual meeting of the Board—the Vice-President in the meantime acting as President pro tem.

A true copy :   E. · R. CRAVEN, *Secretary*.

Extract from the Minutes of The Presbyterian Board of Publication and Sabbath-school Work, in Stated Session, February 26th, 1889.

The Committee appointed at the Special Meeting, February 16th, to prepare a Minute expressive of the views of the Board in reference to the death of its President, the Rev. W. P. Breed, D. D., reported the following, which was unanimously adopted by a rising vote :—

This Board deeply laments the removal by death of its late President, the Rev. William P. Breed, D. D. His long experience in the cause of publication and missionary distribution of religious literature, both before and after the reunion of our Church, well fitted him for the leadership of the body to which that cause was entrusted.

For many years he has stood at our head, a warm, earnest, and intelligent champion of the work of this Board. None of us could excel him in devotion to its interests. Few, if any, gave so much of thought and prayer for its prosperity.

His voice was often raised in its behalf, and his pen put into language many a vigorous appeal for its support.

As an example to follow, and a stimulus to incite, we shall greatly miss his life among us.

His presence and companionship were a benediction. Strong and vigorous, with manly qualities, moved by profound convictions, earnest and bold in his adherence to what he believed to be truth and duty, he was also a tender, gentle, courteous, considerate Christian man, whom none knew but to love and revere.

We have no memories of him which are not fragrant with pleasant thoughts and helpful suggestions towards a better life.

We lay him away from sight, therefore, not to pass out of memory, but ever to be remembered as one of the best of friends, and the wisest of counsellors, as well as a beautiful type of a Christian man and minister.

A true copy :   E. R. CRAVEN, *Secretary.*

Resolutions on the death of the Rev. W. P. Breed, D. D., adopted by the Executive Committee of the Presbyterian Historical Society, Feb. 25th, 1889 :—

WHEREAS, it has pleased God to remove by death Rev. W. P. Breed, D. D., Chairman of the Executive Committee of the Presbyterian Historical Society, Thursday, Feb. 14th, 1889, in the seventy-third year of his age ;

Resolved, That this Committee hereby express their sense of the great loss they have sustained in his removal from the scene of his earthly labors. For a long period he was a member of this Committee and for many years its Chairman, being annually reëlected unanimously. Deeply interested in his work, he was always present at its meetings, when not providentially prevented, and gave his counsel and assistance in the transaction of its business with rare wisdom and judgment. In securing contributions to the Library and the collections of portraits and curiosities, obtaining money to make necessary repairs and improvements in the building, and effecting suitable arrangements for public meetings of the Society, he was unwearied and eminently successful. We realize with heartfelt sorrow, that it will be extremely difficult, if not impossible, to adequately fill the vacancy occasioned by his decease.

Resolved, That we tender our sympathies to the family of Dr. Breed in their severe affliction, and commend them to the grace of the covenant-keeping God, who can sustain in the darkest hour.

Resolved, That a copy of this action be sent to the family of Dr. Breed, published in the religious journals, and engrossed on the Minutes of the Executive Committee.

D. K. TURNER, *Corresponding Secretary.*

Resolutions by the Ministerial Union of Philadelphia, upon the death of Dr. Wm. P. Breed, D. D. Passed March 25th, 1889 :—

At a previous quarterly meeting of the Ministerial Union of Philadelphia, held on December 31st, 1888, Dr. Breed read a paper on "The Propriety of Observing, with Appropriate Religious Services, the Centennial of the Inauguration of the First President of the United States."

This Ministerial Union is composed of the Ministers of the various evangelical denominations of Philadelphia and vicinity.

Upon the occasion when Dr. Breed's paper was read, the Union met in the Hall of the American Baptist Publication Society, 1420 Chestnut Street. The reading was listened to with profound interest by the large assemblage there convened. At the conclusion great applause was expressed, and commendatory remarks thereon were made by prominent men of various denominations, and a large Committee was appointed to devise and suggest a plan for the centennial observance in Philadelphia. Dr. Breed was appointed upon this Committee, and all looked forward in confidence that he would take a leading part in carrying out the celebration in accordance with the enthusiasm which his paper had awakened. But, alas! when the Ministerial Union again came together on March 25th, 1889, in Wesley Hall, 1018 Arch Street, Dr. Breed was greatly missed and mourned over by his brethren. When that Committee to prepare for the Centennial Celebration reported progress, allusion was made to the death of that esteemed one of their number, and the following Resolutions were unanimously adopted by the assemblage:

"*Resolved*, That we are reminded in our meeting, by the absence of our beloved and reverend brother, Dr. Breed, of the fact that in the midst of life we are in death.

"By the sudden ending of the life of this good man and his translation to his heavenly rest, we mourn most of all that we shall see his face on earth no more. We sympathize with the Church in the loss she has sustained in the going out of this great light.

"We tender our sincere condolence with the immediate family, and pray that his mantle may fall upon them and upon his brethren in the ministry of all the Churches.

"*Resolved*, That the officers of this Ministerial Union furnish a copy of this paper to the family of our deceased brother, whose memory we cherish."

The above is a true copy of the action by the Ministerial Union, held on March 25th, 1889.

Signed: ANDREW CULVER,
Secretary of the Ministerial Union.

The following resolution was passed by the Presbyterian Sabbath-school Superintendents' Association, at their meeting held at the Second Presbyterian Church in Germantown, February 18th, 1889:—

Resolved, By the Presbyterian Sabbath-school Superintendents' Association, that in the death of Rev. W. P. Breed, D.D., the Presbyterian Church of Philadelphia and of the country has lost one who will be missed by the entire Church, and particularly by the Presbyterian Church of Philadelphia.

That the Association desire to bear to the family the above as our conviction, and also desire to express our sympathy with the family, believing at the same time that their loss for the time is his gain, and that in the future life they and we will learn to know that God doeth all things well.

And that the Secretary be authorized to convey the same to the family of Dr. Breed.

The above is a true copy from the minutes of the Association.

ROBERT P. FIELD, *Secretary*.

PENNSYLVANIA BIBLE HOUSE,
701 WALNUT STREET, PHILA.,
February 14th, 1889.

MRS. REV. W. P. BREED AND FAMILY.

Dear Friends.—At the stated meeting of the Board of Managers of the Pennsylvania Bible Society, held this day, the death of your esteemed husband and father was officially announced. After a full appreciative expression of the feelings and sentiments of those present, it was unanimously resolved that the President and Corresponding Secretary of our Board be instructed to convey to your stricken and bereaved household the assurance of our heartfelt sympathy and condolence, as also of the genuine regard and fraternal affection entertained for the departed by all his associates.

Dr. Breed was intimately identified with the cause of Bible distribution in our own and in foreign lands, and contributed valuable aid in securing this desirable result.

He was most highly esteemed by all his brethren and co-laborers, for the uniform urbanity and Christian consideration of his intercourse toward all with whom he came in contact.

His memory will be most tenderly cherished by us as that of an able and fearless defender of the plenary inspiration of the word of God, a bright and conspicuous example of its influence in moulding individual character and directing personal aims and ambition, and will be held as an inspiration and impetus in prosecuting the work he loved so well.

We rejoice with you in the rich legacy he has left you of an exalted Christian character and the fruits of a life of untiring activity and usefulness in the Master's service.

We commend you to the Grace of our common Lord and Saviour, and beg you to accept assurances of our personal regard and sympathy.

Very Respectfully Yours,

(Signed)

J. B. DALES, *President.*
W. M. BAUM, *Cor. Secretary.*

At a Stated Meeting of the Executive Committee of the Evangelical Alliance, held on Monday Afternoon, February 18th, 1889, it was—

Resolved, That we have heard with profound sorrow of the death of the Rev. William Pratt Breed, D. D., one of the honored Vice-Presidents of the Alliance since its organization in Philadelphia, and the faithful pastor of the West Spruce Street Presbyterian Church since its foundation.

That in the death of Rev. Dr. Breed, we feel that a Prince and a great man has fallen in Israel; a man who had power with God in his clear apprehension of divine truth; in his faithful presentation of the doctrines of the Gospel of Jesus Christ; in his abounding faith in prayer; in his fidelity as a shepherd and bishop of the flock over which the Holy Ghost made him overseer; in the wisdom of his counsel in all religious organizations, and in the pure and blameless life that marked his ministry in this city for more than a generation.

That in the death of the Rev. Dr. Breed we feel that the Evangelical Alliance as well as the Church Universal and this whole community have suffered an irreparable loss.

That we tender our deepest sympathies to the widow and children of the Rev. Dr. Breed, and pray that the " Father of mercies and God of all comfort " will pour into their hearts the consolations of His all abounding love.

That this resolution be entered on our Minutes, and that a copy of the same be sent to the family of him who, having finished his course in faith, doth now rest from his labors.

	J. H. Hargis,	
Attest :	Lewis H. Redner,	*Committee.*
J. S. Cummings, *Secretary.*	W. A. Selser,	

At the Managers' meeting of the Philadelphia Auxiliary of the American McAll Association, held on Monday, March 4th, 1889, the following Minute was unanimously passed :—

It is with profound sorrow that we record the death of the late Rev. W. P. Breed, D.D., who has been a member of our Advisory Board since the formation of the Auxiliary, and whose past life of holy serving needs no eulogistic words; all who knew him must have felt the power of such a life in all his relationships; truly it was the power of an endless life upon which he has now entered. His gentleness and Christian courtesy towards all were prominent traits in his character, while his broad and well-cultured mind enabled him to be the true friend of all missionary work.

Especially did he respond to the more recent work in the evangelization of France, in whose religious history none were more intelligent, and consequently he was thoroughly alive to the present religious crisis, and the need of persistent effort on the part of Christian America to lay hold of the opportunity of giving the Bible to France. In his death we have lost a true and steadfast friend of our cause, and there will be missed from the world one of its most noble men.

To the stricken family, and the church of his past ministry, we tender our heartfelt sympathies, praying this affliction may prove to lift their hearts heavenward, whither the beloved husband, father and pastor has entered into full fruition of faith.

This Minute shall be placed upon the records of the Auxiliary, and a copy of it transmitted to the family and Presbyterian papers of the city.

By order of the Board of Managers,

MARIA S. EMORY, *Recording Secretary.*

Resolutions of the Directors of the Pennsylvania Institution for the Deaf and Dumb, adopted at a meeting held March 6th, 1889 :—

Resolved, That the Board of Directors of the Pennsylvania Institution for the Deaf and Dumb hereby records the loss that it has suffered by the death of the Rev. William Pratt Breed, D.D., on the 14th of February, 1889, in the seventy-third year of his age. Elected to membership in the Board in the year 1882, he was always willing to devote his time and ability to the performance of his duty ; and during the seven years of his service as Director he endeared himself to all with whom he was brought in contact, by the modesty, kindness and gentleness which were distinguishing traits of his sympathetic nature. By his death the Board has lost a valuable associate, the community an exemplary citizen, and Christianity a tried and faithful advocate.

Resolved, That a copy of this minute be sent to his bereaved family.

JOHN F. LEWIS, *Secretary.*

Letter in *The Evangelist,* of which Dr. Breed was the regular Philadelphia correspondent for many years :—

REV. WILLIAM PRATT BREED, D.D.

BY REV. J. HENRY SHARPE, D.D.

We in the City of Brotherly Love mourn the departure of Dr. Breed as our St. John the Beloved. The light of love was still in his eye and the elasticity of essential youth was still in his step, for he was one whose energies were predominantly spiritual, and these gave their tone to his slight and fragile physique. At threescore years and ten he had still the fire and force of other years, albeit his erect form and fine expressive features had become more spirituelle. We revered and loved him as one whose buoyant bearing and abounding activity seemed to betoken many years more of beneficent leadership in the Church. His sudden departure, therefore, seemed like a transition to the heavenly sphere.

As nearly, perhaps, as ever permitted in our times, Dr. Breed enjoyed an ideal pastorate. Like Dr. Boardman in the Tenth Church, of which the West Spruce Street Church was the child, Dr. Breed grew with the church of which he was the first and only pastor. His previous pastorate at Steubenville, Ohio, had been the novitiate merely, and it was into the second pastorate he poured his still youthful energies. Pastor and people alike were animated by the hopes and aspirations of their untried and promising future. It was the beginning of a pastorate that subsisted unbroken through the average period of human life. The children he baptized in their youth he united in marriage at their maturity. Upon the sons of the fathers whom he followed to their rest he laid the hands of consecration to take the places of their sires at his side. For thirty and three years he ceased not day nor night to minister unfalteringly to this church of his love. He loved it to the end and died in its service.

In every such pastorate the church itself must be one that makes it possible. The West Spruce Street Church was happy in its pastor, and the pastor happy in his church. When his people chose him they were not mistaken in their affinities, and when he became their pastor his affinities for them drew them about him in life-long loyalty. It was a marriage made in heaven, and was to be indissoluble until death. Although the time came when he was forced to demit the arduous responsibilities of other years, he was still retained as pastor-emeritus, and his support continued for life. The action of the congregation in making this provision was a fitting sequel to the memorable occasion of the twenty-fifth anniversary of his pastorate, when the affecting testimony of loving words was substantiated by sharing with him generously in their temporal bounty. Such loyalty to an aged pastor is more an honor to the church capable of it than to the pastor receiving it.

Dr. Breed was too prolific to confine his ministrations to the bounds of his pastorate. He cast a reflected honor on it and on himself by the service he rendered in other kindred spheres. His wise counsel and skillful leadership were in constant demand in the various courts of the Church and in its Boards, and other benevolent agencies. His knowledge of parliamentary practice, his swift perception and decision, his unfailing self-control, his kindly humor and genial tact in every emergency marked him as a model presiding officer, whether in court or in committee. No name was more frequently suggested as fitting for the moderatorship of Presbytery, Synod or General Assembly, and he never failed to acquit himself with honor in such offices as he filled, but it was in the Board of Publication, perhaps, that he rendered his most signal service, being active in all its counsels and its presiding officer since 1876. On countless occasions of greater and lesser moment, as at college and seminary commencements and historic anniversaries, his was a burning and shining light.

His wit and humor were a lambent flame that never failed to play brightly on any theme he treated. Yet few were capable of such touching pathos or of such tender sympathy with the suffering and sorrowing as he. No matter what the occasion, whether joyous or solemn, his spirit ever vibrated truly to its key-note, and responded with an almost feminine fineness of intuition. He had a strong sense of the dramatic in personal character and historic incident, and it was his admiration of noble doing and enduring, rather than philosophic insight, perhaps, that guided him in his historic studies. In picturing the strongest characters and scenes, his pen was more adequate than his voice. Yet he loved to throw himself with an abandon of heroic fervor into the words and actions of his chosen character. At such times his dramatic force often shook his slight frame as if it might shatter it.

It was as a writer, perhaps, rather than as a speaker, that his reputation had the greatest lustre. As his sparkling letters in *The Evangelist* bore witness, he was a born paragraphist. He was a brilliant epigramist. Only grace restrained him from being a punster. A lively fancy was his strongest mental trait. All that he wrote had a charm all its own. His style had the logic of life, and he cared little for any other. His books, tracts, addresses and letters flew to their mark. It is much to say of fugitive writing that it does even this. He had, perhaps, no hope himself that anything he wrote would abide.

Dr. Breed's power was in the manifest purity and intensity of his personal and spiritual affections. His was the heart of St. John, quick to kindle with love, quick to inflame with righteous fervor. If ever he had wrath, it was like his Lord's, only the reflex of his glowing love. His sympathies were so potent he disarmed his opponents without argument, and still won to his good-will those who had to differ with him. He was a dear lover, but a poor hater, and he so loved even his enemies, that they were at peace with him. Love panoplied him from head to foot, and enemies he had none, for he vanquished them into friends. His whole pastorate, as well as his whole history in and out of the church, was a reign of peace as well as purity. His was an unenviable spirit who ever had aught of ill to say of this beloved brother.

This model Christian pastor was fruitful in the vital force that makes force. Not only were there a countless number to attribute their conversion to his saintly influence, but there were many also glad to confess him their father in the Gospel, following in his footsteps to become, like him, heralds of the word of life. Of the two sons who bear his honored name, one of them also treads in his footsteps as a Gospel minister; but perhaps there are a score or more besides, who might rise up to call him blessed of the Lord, because either directly or indirectly he led their feet into the paths of the bearers of glad tidings. From his first Ohio field onward through the long course of his Philadelphia pastorate, he was both the inspirer of young men and their helpful counsellor and friend in all his points of contact with them. Being dead, he yet speaketh through a generation of his spiritual sons, aiming to perpetuate his spirit and the lessons of his life.

Is it any wonder that such a man should have drawn to his funeral services in the church which itself is his enduring monument, a great host of ministerial brethren, and with them many from other denominations? Is it any wonder that not even the wind and rain of the stormy morning hindered a great concourse of all classes to render their homage to the beloved dead ? A life so complete touched both speakers and hearers more with gratitude than with grief. A tribute of tender grateful eulogy pervaded the prayers and addresses alike. All who participated sustained some intimate personal relation to their departed friend. Each of them spoke fittingly, and often eloquently, from his personal point of view, and the whole service was a chaplet of flowers gathered from the choicest in the garden of their hearts. One could only wish that he who so slept under it all might have heard it ere he slept! Alas! why do we refrain from saying what would make a heaven of earth to our loved ones until they have attained to heaven without us!

APPENDIX NOTE.

The following is a list of Dr. Breed's published works.   By the Presbyterian Board of Publication.

No.

12	A Dream,	32mo tract, 8 pp.
828	Anthropos.	Bound Volume
	Bible Lessons on Palestine. *See Question Books,*	" "
641	Book of Books,	" "
1117	Christ Liveth in Me,	" "
1191	Feeding on Christ,	" "
705	Grapes from the Great Vine,	" "
909	Hand-Book for Funerals,	" "
805	Home Songs,	" "
914	Jenny Geddes,	" "
190	John Potter and Uncle Ben,	18mo tract, 4 pp.
675	Lessons in Flying,	Bound Volume
821	Little Priest,	" "
776	Manna Crumbs (*Rutherford*),	" "
52	Man Responsible for his Belief,	18mo tract, 76 pp.
1204	Model Christian Worker,	Bound Volume
1143	Presbyterianism 300 years ago,	" "
1167	Presbyterians and the Revolution,	" "
904	The Prisoners,	" "
768	The Sunny Mount,	" "
64	The Theatre,	18mo tract, 40 pp.
861	Under the Oak.	Bound Volume
1175	Witherspoon,	" "
156	Bridge, The,	18mo tract, 12 pp.
499	Bridget Sullivan,	Bound Volume
1308	Brief, Church History in,	" "
243	Brief Memoirs of the Pious,	" "
1243	Brighter Days,	" "
101-12	British Reformers, (each)	" "
100	British Reformers, Lives of,	" "
137	Brocken, Spectre of the,	18mo tract, 24 pp.
	Broken Basket, The. *See Little Books for Little Readers.*	
1339	Broken Pitchers,	Bound Volume
846	Broken Window,	" "
	Aboard and Abroad. Funk & Wagnalls, New York,	

www.ingramcontent.com/pod-product-compliance
Lightning Source LLC
Chambersburg PA
CBHW020038030726
47499CB00007B/2482